Onion
Ring
theology

CHARLES E. TAYLOR, JR.

Contents

Preface

"We speak of God's wisdom, a wisdom that has been hidden and that God destined for our glory before time began."
I Corinthians 2:7

I've never had an original idea in my life. George Bernard Shaw said it best when he said that all the good ideas were taken by the ancients. So, why does one who never had an original thought presume to write for the benefit of others?

Ideas, like valuable coins handled by many, can become tarnished beyond recognition. They may retain some common utility, but their true value is masked.

In my adulthood, I have become convinced that the ideas of Jesus Christ have been handled by too many careless hands. Stripped of their mystery and passion, they have become common currency in the Western world.

An Oriental acquaintance of mine, upon being exposed to the teachings of Christ, remarked that they are like an onion. When the skin and each successive layer is removed, there remain other rings more pungent and succulent. This is a story of a young college student who dares to peel the onion. In the process, he uncovers a dimension of life without which he could never be complete.

I wrote this book not because I have even one new idea. Rather, I wrote it in the hope of untarnishing a few of the golden coins that God, through Christ, has provided for our benefit.

"Chuck" Taylor
(Originally self-published in April of 1997)

Acknowledgments

An effort like this cannot succeed without help. There are people who deserve my thanks: my wife, Carol, for her encouragement to make this story public. My inspiration for the main character, Doc Masters, is my good friend Larry Hester. Larry's positive approach to life in the face of the challenges of blindness inspires all who know him.

The soft drink *Cheerwine*, mentioned in the text, is a real product. The Twelve Steps referenced in the book are those used in the Alcoholics Anonymous program.

The movie referenced in the book is "Dead Poets Society," released in 1989, by Touchstone Pictures and starring Robin Williams.

The story of Reese Howells, prayer warrior, can be found in a book titled *Reese Howells, Intercessor*, written by Norman Grubb and published by CLC Publishing, 1988.

And, one last big thank you to those who have tolerated my Bible teaching. Teachers always learn more than their pupils.

Crystal Lake

It was a strange caravan that loped along the two-lane country road that Sunday morning. My uncle's huge black Chrysler led the way, towing a pleasure boat equipped with an outboard engine which fidgeted from side to side in front of our Chevy.

The travelers were a happy lot, headed for a week of family fun at Crystal Lake, a strange oasis bubbling up in the midst of flat farmland. The closest we would come to civilization along the way was a research farm owned by the state university. I would have been content to don my bathing suit and play under the giant irrigation system that was treating the corn to a summertime drink. But, it was Sunday and there was duty to be done.

There was a lot at stake. Some of us kids had not missed Sunday school for years. We had the lapel pins chained together to prove it. One for each year. My cousin was shooting for seven straight.

The rules of our Baptist church allowed us to get credit for attending a Sunday school other than our own. I always suspected that the fine print said it had to be at another Baptist church. But this was no time to be reading fine print. We had places to go and things to do.

We had already hit one "dry hole," a Methodist church that for some strange reason held its preaching service at the traditional Sunday school hour. We simply could not spare the time to take in preaching and then Sunday school this day.

As sparse as the population was around those parts, it was not unreasonable to expect a Baptist church around the next curve. Sure enough, there it was. About a football field's distance off the paved road, the white frame church was barely visible through the pines. The sound of singing wafted out windows propped open with tobacco sticks and floated along on what little breeze there was stirring.

Parking a boat is always a problem. We blocked a couple of the cars parked near the church. My uncle probably figured, last in, first out. We wouldn't delay anyone very long.

We men were elected to scout out the situation, while the women waited expectantly in the cars. "We men" included me, my dad, my uncle, my cousin Wesley and his feisty little black and white mutt, Zip. In fact, Zip led the way. Not a good sign! We picked up our pace to keep up with Zip. No chance. The commotion inside the church drew Zip like a magnet to a refrigerator.

Like the windows, the church doors were thrown open wide. Zip trotted in. We followed. We stopped in the vestibule. Zip did not.

At first, I was unsure whether Zip had caused the scene my eyes lit upon. No, Zip was simply reacting to it. Worshippers were waving their hands in the air, throwing their heads back as they shouted, "Amen! Hallelujah! Glory!" These were all Bible words that a ten-year-old recognized. But somehow I couldn't imagine that King James had this in mind. We stood there stunned. All of us, that is, except Zip, who had already joined in the activities down at the altar. He and somebody's grandmother were dancing, hands and paws held high.

About that time a black gentleman with graying hair approached our daddies. "You're welcome to stay and worship with us, sirs. But your dog has got to go!"

One call brought Zip running back up the aisle. One call could have gotten me running back to our car, too. But, we just nodded a polite thank you, turned in unison and reverently made our exit.

We had driven several miles down the road before I could bring myself to ask what was going on in that church. After a protracted silence, without turning his head, my daddy said, "Chad, I suppose the spirit just had hold of 'em."

We laughed about that experience all the way to the lake, except for the time we took to read the Sunday school lesson from our quarterlies. Someday, on the other side, we may find that God didn't really check us off for Sunday school attendance that day. But I'm here to tell you, WE DID!

Doc Masters

With the exception of the times when I laughingly recalled my childhood "spiritual" adventure on the way to Crystal Lake, I thought little about spiritual matters. That is, until I met Doc—I mean Professor Jeremiah Masters. Oh, I attended church as long as I lived in my parents' house. They saw to that, at least until my college days. But exposure at a young age was not enough to make religion "take" in my life.

From the moment I set foot in Doc Masters' biology class, I knew there was something different about this guy. I mean something other than the fact that he was blind. Keep in mind that this was an 8:00 am biology class being taught to a bunch of electrical engineering majors. Unlike me, most of them had not waited until their senior year to take a required freshman course. That fact alone says something about the level of my own excitement for the course.

The point is, this guy Doc Masters was always so happy, I knew he couldn't be for real. His enthusiasm for his subject was infectious. But somehow he taught more than flora and fauna—he taught....life! I mean real-life stuff at eight o'clock in the morning. I couldn't believe it. Everything about this man intrigued me.

Oh, did I mention that Doc was blind? Of course, this meant that he was the brunt of all the typical "no-brain" stunts like hiding his chair and making him search the trays for chalk. I guess that explained why he always carried spare pieces of chalk in his pocket. I never once saw him express anger or frustration at such pranks. He knew how to make you feel okay about his misfortune.

Doc lived alone. I often wondered if he weren't simply a very competent actor, who, when the face paint was removed would become just another miserable, handicapped soul. The truth is, I was haunted by the depth of the sheer joy in his life. I had faced none of the obstacles Doc had obviously encountered in life, yet his joy was foreign to me.

Here I was a senior in college, a fun-loving, woman-crazy guy with his own apartment, a first-class sports car, even a couple of *bona fide* job prospects after graduation. I should be on top of the world.

I guess it was the contrast with my own existence that made Doc Masters look like such a hero to me. Call it jealousy, call it what you will, one day during class I decided it was going to become a part of my education to get inside this man. I was going to find out what made Doc Masters tick.

After that day, I made it a point to be around Doc outside of class. I bugged him during office hours about test papers and homework assignments. He must have thought I was thinking of changing my major. Never once did he fail to give me his full attention. At every encounter, he managed to raise my spirits to a higher plane. After one of those encounters, I was inspired to do a "wild and crazy" thing that cannot be explained with the rational mind. I invited Professor Jeremiah Masters to a movie.

I felt dumb entering the theater with a man sporting a white cane at my arm, and I was glad when they finally turned the house lights off. I had already seen the movie. But there was a special reason I wanted Doc to "see" this film. It was about a zealous, perhaps over-zealous, prep school teacher who encouraged young literature students to live and think freely, to put some passion in their lives. I saw a lot of Doc Masters in this teacher up there on the silver screen. I couldn't wait to sample his reaction to the film.

Afterwards, Doc invited me back to his apartment for wine and conversation. "How do you like Cheerwine?" he asked, sensing my surprise at the cherry-flavored cola he had represented as wine.

"Different," I said, "it's different."

"First timer, huh? It grows on you," he said. Then he beat me to the punch and asked me what I thought of the movie. I told him frankly that I was envious. Envious of the enthusiasm for life, the passion, that the students developed as a result of their encounter with the English professor. I liked the adventure of their secret meetings in the cave. As I went on, I could tell that Doc sensed my thirst for more than Cheerwine.

"Why don't we do it?" he asked.

I sat in stunned silence. "Pardon me," I said, finally coaxing the words out, "do what?"

"Let's you and me find a place in the woods where we can meet and talk about life."

All of a sudden this whole thing seemed a bit kinky. My apprehension must have been apparent.

"Ease up, Chad, I'm a straight guy. And I know by your reputation with the women that you are. Hey, you said you wanted to put some adventure into your life. I know this little shack out at Thurston's mill pond. I'm one of the few people who knows the place. Take a chance, why don't you?"

"Well…okay, how's Saturday afternoon?" I asked, still hesitant.

Doc's response was immediate. "Saturday, at the stroke of midnight and don't tell another soul about this. You'll find a map in an envelope posted on my office door tomorrow. Thanks for the movie. Can you find your way out?"

I could take a hint. I gulped down the last swallow of Cheerwine, grabbed my jacket and left, speechless.

❧

"Do you ever wonder if something really happened or if you just dreamed it? I asked Callie as we sat on the stone wall outside the University library eating burgers. Callie is a girl from my home town. We tell everybody and each other that we're just buddies. However, I must confess to more than one erotic daydream starring the two of us. Her father is a Methodist minister, if that tells you why there's nothing more than dreaming going on.

"What are you mumbling about? You surely have been in a strange mood these last couple of days," she observed.

"Callie, do you realize that we've never had a serious conversation about life?"

"With the mood you're in, I don't think now is the time to have our first one, either. Are you going to eat those French fries?" she asked. "By the way, are we still going to church this Sunday?"

"Ahh….As a matter of fact, I have some very late night plans for Saturday. I'll be sleeping in," I said, remembering my scheduled rendezvous in the woods.

"Okay, be that way," she said. "I'll take my burger and dine alone." And she did.

I admired her legs as she walked away and concluded that she simply wouldn't understand if I had told her my plans. Anyway, I was sworn to secrecy.

∾

The directions had been right where Doc had promised. As I was driving out Route 12 to the mill pond, I realized that I had not even offered to give Doc a lift. How was this blind man going to make his way to a shack hidden in the woods at midnight? Well, I guess the midnight part wouldn't make any difference. Still, Doc had surprised me before. It was easy to forget his handicap.

Let's see, turn off the state road just after the bridge. He's right, this is a rough road. Go about 200 yards. Park in the clearing.

Is this for real? The footpath, the footpath. I should have gotten some new batteries for this flashlight. Every breaking twig sounds like an explosion. I don't know why I'm worried about being quiet, there are only two fools in these woods. At least, I hope there are just two.

"Pssst!"

"Oh God, is that you?" I jumped.

"No, it's just ol' Doc Masters." The voice answered, laughing.

"Doc, that's my heart you're toying with," I complained.

Behind him, my light flashed upon an old lean-to shack. As Doc led me around to the flat side, I spotted the open door which emitted enough light to reveal a pot-bellied stove, a small table holding a gas lantern, and three sagging cane-bottomed chairs, all on a dirt floor. My outstretched arms could have practically measured the radius of the inside.

"Mind if I take my favorite chair?" he asked, bowing at just the right time to avoid hitting his head on the low doorway.

"Feel free," I replied, not really thinking I had surrendered any great treasure. As he sat, I realized that the cane-bottom was form fitting. Doc had been here more than once.

"Well, is this anything like the movie?" he began.

"As a matter of fact, it is. It kinda gets the juices flowing. You know what I mean? And speaking of juices, how about a cold one," I laughed as I pulled two cans of Cheerwine out of the backpack I had brought along.

"Don't mind if I do, friend," Doc replied, grinning as if my gesture had bonded us for life. He leaned his chair back on two legs, sipped some Cheerwine, sighed his satisfaction, and asked, "Who called this meeting anyway?"

"I guess I did, Doc."

"Well then, the dirty floor is yours," he offered.

"I really don't know how to begin, Doc. But you've been so kind to me and you've made me feel so comfortable, and..."

"Spit it out, Chad. There ain't no one here besides you, me and the Good Lord, that is, if he cares to listen in."

"Doc, I've never met a man like you. I sensed from the first day I saw you that you had something that was missing from my life and...dammit, I want to know what it is. No, I want it, period! Tell me how you can live as though you have the world by the tail when God, or whoever, didn't think enough of you to even let you see."

The silence that ensued told me that Doc had been set back by my sudden foray into his private life. He recovered. "It's ironic that you should phrase my physical dilemma in those terms. Because, it was God that used my physical blindness to show me this 'something' that you think I have that you are missing. By the way, I hope you have all night."

"Proceed," I said, inching my chair a bit closer so I could catch Doc's facial expressions in the dim light. "I wasn't always blind," he began. "In fact, I was just a few years older than you, just finished my Ph.D., and working for a research firm out in St. Louis. Flying high, as they say. One day I noticed that my eyesight, which had never been good, was getting blurred. I happened to mention it to my parents in a letter. They wrote back a history of an eye disease called retinitis pigmentosa. The disease had skipped a couple of generations, but obviously it had not skipped me. It always results in blindness.

"Chad, I was devastated. All my life's plan faded before my eyes. In my mind I could picture myself as an invalid, useless to society and to myself.

"The level of my work fell off. I began to drink a lot. And, not Cheerwine either," he said lifting his soda can in the gesture of a toast. "Later, I quit my job to devote full-time to alcohol. It was like God had cheated me out of my inheritance and was going to go down drinking.

"One of those nights when I couldn't make it back to my apartment," Doc continued, "I found myself sleeping on the floor at the Salvation Army. One of the "Hallelujah Hannah's," as they were called, struck up a conversation with me. To her credit, she did not try to save my soul, but she did say something that rang in my head for weeks. She said, 'If you can't see out, why don't you try to see in?'

"Within the next few months, I was almost totally blind. One night, I was really considering doing the world and myself a big favor and ending the whole farce. But I couldn't get Hannah's words out of my mind. 'If you can't see out, why don't you try to see in?' It was then that I said out loud: 'Alright, God, I'm looking inside. Now show me something.' That moment, in my mind's eye I could see an old hymn book we used when I was a little boy. It was open to page 163. The words, the notes, they were all there. I began to sing, 'Amazing grace, how sweet the sound, that saved a wretch like me. I once was lost but now am found, was blind, but now I see.'"

Doc's blind eyes filled with tears. He licked one as it passed his mouth. "Son," he said to me, "when you can see what I can see, then you'll have what I have."

It was difficult for Doc to form those words. I waited in silence while he used a swallow of Cheerwine to wash down the lump in his throat. He continued, "Unfortunately, as hard as it was for a blind man like me to see it, it is even harder for a man like you with two good eyes."

Needless to say, Old Chad was not prepared for this heavy stuff. Maybe a little worldly philosophy, but not this. I did gather the presence of mind to ask Doc if he would tell me what he saw, adding that, perhaps, someday I just might be able to see it for myself.

Doc went on about how he simply asked God to forgive him for the life he was wasting. He asked God to show him how even a life like his could be lived out successfully. Doc told me how he would go down to the Salvation Army and get Hanna to read the Bible to him. Then he would go home and ask God to show him what it all meant. He would just wait on God to bring it to his mind's eye. Most often, the explanation would come in the form of some mental image of nature. He assumed that was because it was what he knew best.

On one such occasion, Hannah had read to him where Jesus Christ (Doc was careful to make sure that I knew who he was) said that he was a vine and that humanity formed the branches. Doc confessed that the vine and branch was a very difficult concept for him to grasp. The wait was longer than usual. But when the insight came, it revolutionized his life.

At that point, Doc reached into his coat pocket and pulled out, what else, a piece of chalk. His free hand reached out for the flat siding that formed the inside wall of the shack. Using the siding of the shack wall as a chalkboard, he proceeded to draw some sort of crude picture or diagram. "This will only take a minute," he said.

I took the occasion to stumble around back of the shack to take a whiz.

"Don't 'pee' on the wood pile," Doc yelled. In fact, we could use a log or two in the stove. We might be here for a while."

I stumbled back inside, wood in hand, bumping my head on the door frame as I entered.

"Okay, Chad, I'm ready now. This is Spiritual Botany 101."

Using his chalk diagram, Doc refreshed my fading memory about certain kinds of plants that have rhizomes. He reminded me that most people think rhizomes are roots, but they are not. Rhizomes are underground stems or vines and the plants that shoot above the surface are really branches from the rhizome, the invisible vine. Each branch may eventually develop its own root system and live independently from the vine which runs, unseen, underground. At least the branches appear to live independently, until the cold of winter kills back the foliage and the branch is forced to look inward, below the ground, for its sustenance.

"Chad, picture Jeremiah Masters as a branch unaware of the subterranean vine that had actually given him life. Unaware, because he had learned to use his own physical senses: hearing, smelling, touching, tasting, and yes, seeing, to interact with his environment. Within him are natural drives that move him to feed and protect himself. These physical senses and drives not only help him survive, they bring him pleasure. Bear with me here, Chad. I know I'm stretching the analogy," Doc interjected.

13

Then he continued. "Jeremiah discovers that some foods are better than others. He discovers that a home can be not only a safe place, but a cozy place, a comfortable place. In fact, Jeremiah Masters realizes that he could live his entire life depending merely upon his physical senses. Many of his fellow plants subscribe to the philosophy, 'If it feels good, do it.' Their leaves are green and shiny, their stems are robust, the gentle rains and warm breezes of spring and summer invigorate them. They are really livin'!

"But, alas, Jeremiah Masters grows weary of this life. He desires more than an existence. He discovers that under the surface of his branch there is activity. There is an inner part of Jeremiah Masters. He can acquire and store knowledge, he has feelings, deeper feelings than the simple responses associated with his senses. He discovers that he is not a slave to his physical drives. He can make independent decisions. Although he has a physical appearance resembling those plants near him, he realizes that he is an individual, he is 'his own plant.'

"Jeremiah now has everything working for him—his healthy body to interact with his environment and his alert mind, a determined will and controlled emotions with which to direct his life. Yet, when he is honest with himself, he does not feel complete. There is more to Jeremiah Masters than he can discover.

"He is maturing. Those gentle breezes are now sometimes replaced by gusts that buffet his leaves and test his branch. His leaves begin to lose their vitality and their sensitivity. They change color. His bark thickens. It becomes more important to him that his life make some kind of difference. He needs a purpose for being. Jeremiah deepens his intellectual search, reaching to the very point where his branch meets the soil. He wonders if there is any of himself below this earthen barrier.

"One day, Jeremiah Masters faces disaster. Suddenly, he is terribly cold, his leaves fall from their connections, he can no longer interact with the environment. He takes temporary solace in the fact that he has developed a life within himself. He wonders how his friends who chose to lead a completely physical existence have fared. Not well, he speculates. His own comfort is short-lived. His intellect, his will, his emotions are not equal to the crisis. He feels his very life hanging in the balance.

"It is useless to exist, he thinks. That moment, he feels a pressure from below the surface. It is as if a foreign force is pushing to enter his being. He can remember this pushing as a faint sensation, easily overcome in his stronger days. But now, this crisis has weakened him to the point of vulnerability. The risk to his individuality, to his selfness, seems monumental. But strangely, he senses that his salvation might just lie in surrender to this force. Jeremiah's intellect advises against it, his emotions resist. His physical senses shut down. But at the very base of his being, he allows his will to surrender.

"What happens at that point defies description. At first, there is warmth oozing into the void. Then, his being is overwhelmed with this force that is at once powerful and gentle. It envelops, it invigorates, it…loves. There is peace, not at all explainable, but real. And, to Jeremiah's amazement, this force does not war with the forces that had resisted it. He discovers that his individuality is not compromised. Rather, for the first time in his life, Jeremiah feels…complete. There was a source, much greater than himself, which wanted to fill the void in Jeremiah's being. It wanted to give expression of itself through him. Jeremiah was happy to oblige. There was a new relationship, a new life, a oneness with this force from deep within himself. There was purpose in his being. Jeremiah was connected—connected with something greater than himself."

There was an extended silence. Doc's hand searched to touch me as if to assure my undivided attention. I shifted my shoulder so that his hand would find its mark.

"Chad, I've got news for you. What you are in search of, you will never grasp with your physical senses. Neither will you fathom it with your intellect, nor contact it with your emotions. These very faculties which you have worked to develop during your few years are simply insufficient to make you a complete person. In fact, they represent barriers between you and the completeness you seek. You and I, and all humanity, must recognize that there is a force beyond our conscious selves, greater than ourselves, hidden deep within ourselves, without which we can never be whole.

"Hannah had encouraged me to look inside myself to discover the source of my wholeness." Doc's hand reached for the wall again. This time it located the door. With a swift push, Doc flung the door wide open. The sound of the squeaky hinges and the swinging latch took a few seconds to subside. Meanwhile, my eyes feasted upon the mill pond lit by a harvest moon.

"What is deep within us is a door," Doc continued, "a door which only we can open. The force is behind this door. It manifests itself by invitation only.

"Chad, can you picture this peaceful scene actually moving through the open door, becoming a part of you?"

For an instant, my mind had to process the question of how Doc could know what scene I was viewing. How could he know how softly the moon's reflection lay upon the still water? Without an answer, my mind moved on to consider Doc's question. "Yes, seeing this scene makes me feel peaceful," I replied.

"Not good enough, Chad. Your senses are still controlling. You're reacting to what you see. Invite it in."

Invite it in, I coached myself. My eyes closed. The visual image was still there. It really was still there. It was like I had captured it. It was mine. I could carry that peaceful scene with me beyond the moment.

Doc spoke. "One of Walt Whitman's poems begins: 'A child went forth, and everything he touched, that thing became a part of him.' Chad, when you deliberately open the door of your spirit, what you see will become not just an experience, but a living part of you."

Doc paused to allow my mind to take it all in. Honestly, the best I could do was file it away for another time. Then, Doc asked if I owned a Bible.

"No, but I can get my hands on one," I shrugged.

"Good, here's a homework assignment for you. In the Bible find the book called John. Keep the spiritual botany lesson you just heard in the back of your mind while you read the entire book. Ignore the details you don't understand and focus on the concepts that are being communicated. You can tell me what you have learned at the next Society meeting."

"What society meeting?" I asked.

Doc grinned, "I'm calling a meeting of the 'S.O.B.'s for next Tuesday, same time, same station."

"Doc, quit talking in riddles. Who are the S.O.B.'s?"

"The Society of Believers, of course. And just in case you are not initiated by then, I'm bringing along a couple of other believers. After all, one person can't be a society by himself. Guess what? You've got to take me home. It's way past my bedtime."

I remembered how inconsiderate I had been by not offering Doc a ride out to this place. "Doc, I completely forgot that you needed a ride out here. How did you get here?"

"Connections, Chad," he answered, "I've got connections."

The S.O.B.'s

Callie wasn't impressed when I called her Sunday afternoon to ask if she would lend me a Bible. I knew she had more than one and I thought she'd be proud that I was seeking the "straight and narrow."

"Chad Clayborn, you've got a lot of nerve," she began. "You stay out so late on Saturday night with one of your lady friends that you can't go with me to church. Then, you try to butter me up by making me think you're interested in what the Bible has to say."

"But…"

"Don't you 'but' me, Chad Clayborn," she continued. Obviously, I think a lot more of God's word than you do of me. Well, you listen to me! I don't intend to be another notch on your belt. If I never see you again it will be too soon."

"Now, Callie, is that any way for a Christian to act?" I countered.

"Well, no. But sometimes you make me lose what little religion I've got."

Click%#@]% In case you're wondering, that was the phone slamming. That hurt my ear! But not nearly as much as it hurt my heart. Doesn't Callie understand that I know she's not like all those other girls? Doesn't she understand that I would never do anything to hurt her? I guess not.

I clicked on the TV. It was preset on the all-sports channel. I got an English soccer match. Whoopee. I lay on the bed as the British announcer called the play-by-play action. My mind leaped back and forth between the wonderful things I had heard at the Society meeting, the death sentence I had been handed by Callie, and the blasted soccer match. I had gotten up to rid my mind of the latter distraction when I heard the announcer say something very unexpected.

The team in blue was pushing the ball down the field for a shot on the goal. As one of the forwards booted the ball towards the net, the announcer shouted, "Oh no, he sinned!"

I stared at the screen, hoping to detect the violation. To my surprise there was no foul. As always, the "instant replay" followed. "Look at this," the announcer said with emphasis. "Parsons had a clear shot on goal and he sinned high and off to the left."

I watched as the ball did indeed sail past the goal, high and to the left. But how did Parsons sin? This announcer guy was using a Bible word that I was sure had gone out with King James himself. I had never heard the word "sin" used in a context other than to describe wrongdoing. Obviously, it meant something different in soccer. The announcer was using the word sin to point out that the player had missed the goal.

I didn't have a Bible, but I sure as heck had a dictionary. There it was, the word was of English origin and one meaning was to miss the goal or mark. "Well, I'll be," I remarked to myself. And, myself answered, "Yes, you are." Right then, all by my lonesome, for the first time in my life, I realized that *I was a sinner*. Oh, I was not an alcoholic like Doc. Not by a long shot. But, brother, I had missed the mark big time. Everything Doc had said the night before came back to me. I realized that I had completely closed God out of my life. All I could say was *God, forgive me, I have missed the mark*. I said it over and over.

Call me crazy, but I felt the same kind of pushing from within that Doc had described. Like Jeremiah, the plant, my reason and feelings told me to "get over it." There was a war going on inside me.

I needed to tell somebody about this. Callie? No, she won't believe me. Doc? He told me some friends were taking him to the lake for the day. There was no one who would understand. Look, this can't be happening to me. I haven't even read the Bible yet. That's what I'll do. The mall is open on Sunday. There's a bookstore there. They're bound to sell Bibles. After all, they say it's the world's best seller.

Later that afternoon, and into the evening, I read the book of John as Doc had suggested. I read how this guy, Nicodemus, had come at night to Jesus Christ for some answers. Kinda like I came to Doc Masters.

Jesus told him that he had to be "born again," born of the spirit. Nicodemus had the same problem I did with that concept. What spirit? How can this be?

As I read on, Jesus spoke about how God would send a spiritual counselor that would teach men what they needed to know about God. I pictured Doc playing that role in my life.

I read the part where Christ compared himself to the vine, and his disciples to the branches. As I read the words, keeping in mind Doc's biology lesson, I realized that Jesus Christ had come to earth to introduce this supernatural force to men. He called it abundant life. Our job is to open the door to his message, to allow it to become a part of us.

All of this I could understand intellectually. But it was like viewing the moonlit pond through the door. I knew it was not yet a part of me.

It was late now. I decided not to call Doc. I would have plenty of questions for him at the Society meeting Tuesday night. I decided not to try to contact Callie either. Maybe I could talk to Doc about her.

If I went to class on Monday and Tuesday, I don't remember anything about it. My entire being was totally occupied with this inner struggle. The only thing that was clear to me at this point was that there had to be some resolution. Something had to remove this paralysis.

All I remember is that Tuesday midnight could not have come too soon. Driving out, I recalled that Doc said there would be others there. Sure enough, my car's headlights revealed another car parked in the clearing at the end of the path. In the opening I could see the charred ruins of a building of some kind. I supposed it was a farm house out in front of the mill.

Spotting the footpath more easily than before, I brushed by several saplings and toward the small light I could now see in the distance. I shone my flashlight on the shack door. Overhead was a wooden hanging sign inscribed with the letters "S.O.B." It had not been there before. I had to duck my head to miss it, but at least I didn't bump my head on the door this time.

"It worked, Doc," a voice said.

Lifting my head, I saw three old geezers staring at me. Well, two were really staring. I always forgot about Doc's blindness.

"Well, you made it, Chad. And you didn't even bump your head. Good job, Batty." Doc was addressing a wiry black man with gray hair, who rose slightly from his seat and extended his hand.

"Hey son, I'm Bartholomew Battle. Folks just call me Batty. I don't take offense to it.

"Hello, Batty," I replied. I've never heard that nickname before.

"You've never known anyone like Batty before, either," the other old gentleman said. "I'm Thomas Morehead. I would offer you my seat, but you can handle that floor much easier than I can." Thomas Morehead was a stately white-haired white guy with a ruddy complexion who appeared to be big enough to make two of Batty. I liked his easy smile.

"Chad, we started to bring another chair, but since we weren't sure you would be a regular, we decided to save ourselves the trouble. The ground isn't that hard."

"No problem, Doc. Those chairs look like they fit you guys better than they would me anyway. Doc, I have something to ask you."

"It will have to wait a couple of minutes. We were about to take the Society's oath. Batty is leading us. Go ahead, Batty." Batty fumbled with what appeared to be some pages from a book or magazine. As he lifted the pages close to his face, I could read the backside from my seat below him. Copyright 1952, 1953, 1981 by the A.A., Grapevine, Inc. and Alcoholics Anonymous Publishing. I had already heard Doc's confession of alcoholic addiction. I wondered if this was a real A.A. meeting. If so, I had no place here. A few social drinks do not qualify one for that "Society."

As he began, I realized that Batty was paraphrasing what was on the sheet. *"I admit that I am powerless over sin—that my life has become unmanageable."* There was that word "SIN" again.

"I do," chimed in both the others.

Batty continued, *"I believe that a Power greater than myself can restore me to sanity."*

"I do."

"I do," Tom said, getting out of sync.

"I have decided to turn my will and my life over to the care of God as I understand Him."

"Amen," nodded Thomas Morehead.

"I do," said Doc with his head bowed.

"I do too," I surprised myself and everyone there by speaking up. My heart was pounding, "I'm serious. Doc, I just realized that I can say 'I do' to all three of those statements."

I could see those men's faces begin to beam. Instantly I felt the warm flow that Doc had described in his spiritual biology lesson. It was a new sensation that I could not describe. Words seemed inadequate and unnecessary. This was spiritual communication. I was among kindred souls.

Finally, I spoke. "Doc, I must admit that your life's story is so different from my own that I found it hard to equate the sin in your life with my own. I thought maybe I just hadn't lived long enough to get in the kind of trouble you were in. As a matter of fact, I was quite proud of myself. That is until I found out that sin was simply missing God's intention for my life. All the things I pictured as sin were just symptoms."

Doc broke in, addressing the other two, "You see, fellas, I keep telling you, the reason there are so few true believers is that the message Jesus Christ came to bring has simply been distorted beyond recognition."

I was the one who responded. "Hold it Doc. I don't follow you."

"Well, Chad, it's true I had to hit rock bottom before I recognized my need for help from a power greater than myself. But, it doesn't have to be that way. You are living proof of that. In Alcoholics Anonymous we practice a technique called 'raising the bottom.' That's a term for helping problem drinkers recognize that they don't have to hit bottom before they can be helped by that 'Greater Power.' We try to get them to see that the 'Power' can halt their slide before alcohol destroys their life. Believers need to educate people about sin like A.A. educates people about alcohol. Chad, you've mastered lesson number one. Be-lievers call it repentance. To repent is to realize that you're head-ed in the wrong direction and it's necessary to turn around."

"Okay, Teach," I chimed in, "I'm ready for lesson number two."

After I shut up, Batty continued the oath, *"I have made a searching and fearless moral inventory of myself."* After the "I do"s, I admitted that my inventory was far from complete, but that I had started. Batty said that their inventories weren't complete either, but we would deal with that later.

As Batty moved through the remaining steps of the pledge, which was obviously meant for alcoholics, I marveled at how appropriate each step was to my own life. It did not take a genius to see that these guys were using the steps as some kind of spiri-tual road map. They were using them to reaffirm the direction of their lives and encouraging each other to "stay the course."

After Batty finished, I spoke. "I need that list. It's just what I need to follow."

"It really is," Doc agreed. "But there is a danger in trying to do God's will by the numbers. Why don't you just take it one step at a time? Chad, it's easy to say intellectually that you believe in a power greater than yourself. It is another matter altogether to place your will and your life under the control of that power. Don't you agree?"

"Well, yes, Doc. But I'm feeling really good about all this. Isn't that a positive thing?"

"And a very necessary first step, Chad. Fellas, I think Chad is ready for a little spiritual quiz. Doc looked back and forth between big Tom and little Batty. "Batty, the first word please."

"Uhhhh…" Batty strung it out while he was thinking. "After repentance comes faith. Yeah, faith. Chad, do you know what having faith in God means? I must have looked so puzzled that

Batty hardly hesitated. "It means more than believing God exists. Faith is believing that trusting God will make a difference in your life now and eternally."

"Is that eternal, as in for all time?" I asked.

"Actually, eternal implies beyond time as we know it," Doc replied. "But the important point here is this. Do you remember our spiritual biology lesson, the rhizome and the branch? The branch might have believed that the rhizome had the power to provide new life for the branch. But it was only when the branch acknowledged its own inadequacy and allowed the rhizome's life-giving force to occupy it that the new life became a reality. Trusting God will bring the same new life experience. Stand up, Chad."

I struggled to my feet, feeling more than a bit awkward. "Have you ever seen a mime who could give the appearance of leaning on an invisible post?" Doc asked.

"Yeah, sure," I said, quickly striking the pose as best I could.

Tom entered the conversation. "A good mime is very convincing. Right?"

"You mean I'm not?"

"Lean more," Tom suggested.

I was teetering as it was. "I can't. I'll fall on my face." I did in fact lose my balance and clumsily eased myself to a sitting position.

Tom continued, "Chad did you sense the point at which you realized that to lean one more degree would mean that you would lose control?"

"Yes, you feel very vulnerable," I observed.

"Precisely." Batty took his turn. "When you are leaning on God, you feel exactly that way. At least, in the beginning."

"Chad, remember how Jesus described God's spirit to Nicodemus in the book of John that I suggested you read?" Doc asked.

"Something like the wind blows but you can't tell where it comes from or where it's going. He said God's spirit is like that," I answered, feeling a bit of pride at just recalling those words.

"And so it is, Chad. You must put your trust in that which you cannot see. Only when you get to the point when you truly release control will you find that you are leaning on what the Scriptures call the Everlasting Arms. That is spiritual faith."

"Well, I do sorta feel that way now, but what I hear you saying is that this leaning must be a way of life."

"Excellent, this boy has potential!" exclaimed Batty.

"Sin, repentance, faith, what's next, Tom?" Doc asked, continuing to play his role as quiz show host.

"Chad," Tom began, "do you remember how you felt when you answered 'I do' to that third question about turning your will over to God?"

"Yeah, I still have that feeling. There is a peace that was not there before," I confessed.

"When you exercised your faith, you triggered the next quiz word, grace. What do you know about grace, Chad?"

"Well, this isn't spiritual, but I know when I see a graceful dancer. Am I getting warm?"

"You're really closer than you might think," Tom said. "Let's look at your example. Do you agree that it is possible for a dancer to practice to the point of knowing all the mechanical moves of dance and yet lack that certain something that makes her a complete dancer?"

"Ahh, yeah...sure," I replied, after a moment's hesitation.

Tom continued. "Then would it be safe to say that there is an unexplainable, even mystical, quality in some dancers which so complements their mechanical skills that they seem complete?"

"Right, and that unexplainable something is grace!" I exclaimed.

"You've just defined spiritual grace. It is the spiritual power to be complete. It is the gift of God that allows us to please Him, just as the graceful dancer pleases her audience."

"Well, Chad," Batty spoke up, "you're down to the final word in this spiritual vocabulary quiz. When by your faith you allow God's spirit to fill your life with grace, you begin to experience salvation. Chad, this one is for all the marbles. Define salvation." Doc, always the comedian, sang out "dum, dum, dum, dum," indicating I was running out of time.

"Well, I always thought it meant like you were snatched from sin and its consequences."

"What do you think, fellas?" Batty surveyed the other two judges.

"He's not completely wrong," Doc said, offering me the benefit of the doubt.

"You're right, Doc," Tom joined in. "But being snatched from sin is only a by-product of salvation. This is for the grand prize. He's gotta do better," Batty agreed.

"Okay, okay," I broke in. "How's this?" I knew this was a real stretch, but I went for it. "If grace is the power to be complete and salvation comes by grace, then salvation must be completeness or wholeness." There was silence as the judges looked at each other. The longer they stared, the dumber I felt.

Then Doc announced, "Gentlemen, meet the champion of the spiritual vocabulary quiz. Congratulations, Chad. You're the newest member of the S.O.B.'s!"

"Doc, are you serious?"

"Sure. If you truly believe that these few spiritual words describe the experience you have had, then you are a Christian and our brother."

"But I know so little. I'm not really complete," I confessed.

"Well, in all honesty, Chad, neither are we," Tom explained.

"Salvation is a process, not just an experience. As we allow God's grace to penetrate every facet of our lives, we become more and more like Christ, who was and is complete because he is 'full of grace.' Doc, I think it's time for Chad's Spiritual Anatomy lesson."

"I don't think so, fellas. It's getting late and we've really put Chad to the test tonight. Chad, why don't you stop by my class tomorrow around three and I'll lay the anatomy lesson on you and throw in a spiritual geography lesson to boot."

"That sounds good to me, Doc. Guys, you don't know what this experience means to me."

"Oh, yes we do," Batty said. "Each of us has been where you are. Each of us had someone to help us understand sin and repentance and faith and grace and salvation. We know exactly what it means. That's why we're so happy to have you as a brother in the S.O.B.'s."

Walking away from that shack and leaving the presence of those men was like leaving "holy ground." It wasn't just what I had learned from them, it was something extra, something mystical; it was grace. Amazing grace!

Onion Rings

Taking a personal moral inventory is not a pleasant task. Now, I have taken inventories before. My father owns a furniture store and taking inventory comes with the territory. But in the store there's always a list. Chest: Walnut, four-drawer, with brass hardware. Simple—either you have it or you don't.

Not so with personal inventories. What are you looking for? How many people did you murder today? How many sports cars did you covet? How do you get outside yourself so that you can make an accurate, objective assessment? Who knows?

This was the tone of the conversation I was having with myself as I walked across campus to Moore Hall where Doc Masters was finishing his class lecture. The moral inventory thing and thoughts of Callie had been competing for my conscious attention all day.

It's ironic that I've "gotten religion" like Callie wanted me to, and I can't tell her because she won't understand. Well, I may not have her kind of religion. Callie is a traditionalist—church on Sunday morning, Sunday night and again on Wednesday. Don't do this. You must do that. Believe everything I believe or you aren't a believer at all. There is something claustrophobic about Callie's kind of religion.

Doc's religion is not like that. I mean, they both have Jesus Christ at the center, but Doc's religion lets you breathe. There is freedom. It's not a bunch of rules…it's a relationship thing.

Thinking of relationships, this whole Callie thing bothers me. There doesn't seem to be any physical chemistry between us. Hey, that's not my fault. Believe me, I've tried! And there's no intellectual common ground. Lately, she won't let the conversation get beyond why I'm not willing to go to church with her. But still, I have an attraction to Callie which I cannot explain. Could she be right? Is it just the attraction of forbidden fruit? If not, what's the attraction? I wish I knew what it was. Frankly, it's worrying the hell out of me.

Slumping down beside the wall across from Doc's classroom, I can see and hear the blind man. He has his students on their mental tiptoes as usual. All the while he's fiddling with a piece of paper. Slowly, he walks toward the open door, still lecturing. Lifting his arm, he sets sail a paper airplane. It zooms out the door directly toward me like it's equipped with a homing device. I have to duck to avoid being pinned against the wall by the dumb thing. How did he know I was out here? Sometimes I really think his blindness is a hoax.

The airplane has a message written on the wing. "Two you-know-whats, down the hall to the left." Two whats? Nothing to do but trek down the hall and try to decode this clandestine message from the blind, crazy professor. At the end of the hall is an alcove with a vending machine. This must be the only soft drink machine in the world that vends Cheerwine. I can't believe it! Doc must have refused to teach in this building unless his favorite beverage was readily available.

Here I stand with two cans of Cheerwine as students file out of Doc's class. One guy I recognize gives me the old "Oh, you shouldn't have" as he grabbed for one of the cans. I was too quick for him.

Last to leave was Debby Sanders. I remember Debby; man, do I remember Debby! She gave me one of her naughty smiles. My eyes naturally followed her out the door. For once, I was glad Doc could not see everything.

"Miss Sanders is an attractive young lady isn't she, Chad?" The good Doctor surprised me. "Close the door. Thanks for the refreshment," he said gratefully, popping the top on his Cheerwine. "What kind of day have you had?"

"Pensive," I replied, feeling good that I had chosen a single word that actually summarized my day. "I've been trying to sort through all that 'believer's stuff' you guys threw at me last night. And then there's Callie."

"Oh, is she your latest mark?" Doc quizzed.

"Doc, please, give me a break," I pleaded. "This one is different."

"How so? A real challenge, huh?" Doc grinned.

"More than a challenge; my ear is still ringing from the phone she slammed down last Sunday. Can we change the subject?"

"Sure, have a seat. No, I have a better idea. Do you like hamburgers?"

"Doc, I'm a college student. What do you think?"

"Yeah, well, let's walk over to the library snack bar. Batty makes the best burger in town," Doc said, grabbing his white cane off the tabletop on his way out the door. "I missed lunch. I'm starved."

"Batty?" I questioned, trying to catch up to Doc's quick pace. "You mean the black guy from the Society meeting?"

"Oh, is he black?" Doc quipped. "Yeah, that was Batty. He's the reason the Society meets at midnight. He has worked the

3-to-11 shift at the snack bar for years. It used to be a second job, but he quit his day job a while back. Retired. He's an institution around here. You must have seen him before. The snack bar is just next door to the library."

"Doc, is that a comment on my study habits? I do my library studying on the day shift, okay?"

"Changing the subject," Doc said, "how are you coming with your moral inventory Chad?"

"Yeah, well," I stumbled, "I frankly couldn't get to first base. I really thought you might offer a few pointers."

"Well, Chad, it probably wasn't fair to assign you the task of taking a moral inventory quite yet. The fact is, you can't take such an inventory by yourself. You'll need help from someone you don't really know yet. But, before you meet him, you will probably benefit from some more spiritual training. And that will have to wait until I get my hands on that hamburger."

We made small talk the rest of the walk from Moore Hall to the library snack bar. As we entered the door, Batty welcomed us from behind the counter. "Well, look what the blind man drug in. Doc, I'm glad to see you keeping such high-class company. Hey, Chad! Good to see you in the daylight."

I could only manage a nod before Doc's comeback. "Do you always greet your customers so warmly?" he asked in feigned sarcasm.

Batty shot back, "Only those I love, Doc. Only those I love and those who can't see how to chase me down. And you fall into both categories."

Doc just shook his white cane in Batty's direction. "Get busy, old man. We want two burgers, all the way," he said, turning his head toward me for confirmation.

"Ahh…that's fine," I said, finally catching up with the conversation.

"Oh," Doc added, "and bring us an order of those onion rings I smell cooking."

Doc escorted me to a corner booth away from the small crowd that had congregated near the grill where Batty had several short orders sizzling.

A moment later, Batty was coming toward us with a tray of food. "And will you gentlemen be having wine with dinner? Let me recommend the house wine. It has a sweet, fruity flavor." As he spoke, Batty plopped two 'you-know-whats' on the table. I had just discarded my last one in the garbage can outside the snack bar. I wasn't sure I could handle another just yet. Doc had not even finished his. None of this mattered to Batty, who had already decided that Cheerwine was our beverage of choice. "And your piping hot onion rings," Batty continued. "I just happened to be frying a new batch when you came in. Will there be anything else for you this evening?"

Doc continued the formal tone of the conversation. "My good man, my extraordinary sense of smell tells me that you have delivered just what the doctor ordered. That will be all for now, thank you."

Batty rolled his eyes for my benefit and left without a final rebuttal.

Doc felt for the basket of onion rings. His fingers found a small one. He popped it in his mouth. "Hot," he managed to utter as he swallowed. "I recommend that you wait a minute before sampling Batty's greasy cuisine.

"Chad, Tom and Batty are always teasing me about my spiritual mini-lessons. You don't mind if I give you one while we wait for the burgers, do you?"

"No, Doc. Remember, that's why I came."

"Okay then. I'll need your help. Find the largest onion ring in the basket and place it on a napkin." This I did with puzzled hesitation.

Doc continued his instructions, "Now, find a smaller one that fits inside the larger one, and a really small one for the very center."

This task was not as easy as it would seem, but I finally found three that formed concentric circles. I acknowledged my success. "All done."

"Great," Doc said. "The rest of the onion rings are yours. I'll talk, you eat."

This seemed like a favorable division of labor. I pulled the basket closer and prepared to listen.

"What you are going to hear and see will seem like a huge oversimplification, Chad, and some of this will be a review of my plant story. Please bear with me." Doc paused to gather his thoughts. "I think you will agree that a human being can exist on several levels. For example, there's the purely physical existence." Doc fingered the large outer onion ring, peeling a bit of its batter away. "By using your senses and certain basic drives, you can interact with the environment around you at a basic subsistence level. You use your hearing, touching, smelling (Doc fanned the onion smell away), tasting, and most folks even use their sight, to function on this level.

"Also, there are certain instinctive drives, such as the desire for food, for protection from harm, for propagation (he smiled) and so on. These are associated with hormones which people possess in greater or lesser degrees, a fact to which you are testimony. But they normally appear in all of us. In this regard, we are like all animals.

"It is possible to exist with only these basic endowments. But the operative word is 'exist.' You might be able to cite examples of people who spend their lives 'living' at the purely physical level, gratifying these basic desires. Sometimes we say these people live like animals. Most of us have learned that there is more to life. In fact, we consider people who live at this level uncivilized. Do you agree?"

"I'm with you, Doc."

"Well then, Chad, what makes one civilized?" Doc asked, probably thinking he needed to involve me more in this lesson before boredom overcame me.

"It's kinda the idea that men and women have to cooperate with each other. So...so they use their minds to control some of these instincts for the good of those around them."

"Well said, Chad. We do have the capacity to transcend the purely physical—we have minds." Doc picked up the next largest ring and turned it as if he were examining it with his eyes. "Not just brains, but emotions and that special something within us we call our will. We might say that civilized people use their minds and emotions to influence their will and to exercise control over their more basic instincts. In fact, the use of these faculties is what distinguishes us from the other animals, and from each other; so that we say we have individual personalities."

Doc continued, "So now we have common instincts, differing mental capacities and individual emotions all vying to prevail over this part of us we call our will. For example," he paused to inhale the aroma of the onion rings, "we smell our favorite food, our mouth waters, our emotions surrender, but our brain says 'no, it's too fattening.' So we don't eat it. Chalk one up for reason."

That comment caught me in mid-bite. It took an extra swallow to get the onion ring I was devouring to go all the way down.

"But reason is not always the winner," Doc went on. "Sometimes we know a certain decision is not correct intellectually, but it feels good, so reason is overridden. You are providing a perfect example of overridden reason right now."

All of a sudden, I lost my taste for onion rings and pushed the basket aside.

"The point is, Chad, while the will can be influenced by any and all of these physical, mental or emotional factors, it is really independent of them.

"Now, you see, men and women have been given the tools to successfully interact with their physical environment, and with each other. And just as some choose to live life on the purely physical level, most people seem content to add their minds, that is, their intellect and emotions, to the equation. They seem happy to interact with the world around them and with other humans with some degree of civility."

"But, Doc, you have a circle left over," I said, referring to a small innermost onion ring.

"Okay, Chad. If the senses and instincts provide our interface with the physical world, and the mind provides an interface with the rest of humanity, what must this final circle represent?"

"An interface with interplanetary life?" I threw out a wild guess.

"No, the astronauts and cosmonauts are proof that man can transcend his own little earth by using his body and mind."

"Then, we're talking about another dimension?" I pondered out loud.

"Precisely, and what might that dimension be?" Doc prompted. I voiced the words sheepishly, "Would it have something to do with God?"

"It has everything to do with God, Chad. It is our interface with our Creator. It is our spirit. Listen, all of life can be defined with one word—relationship. We know we are physically alive because we have a relationship with the physical world. But, if someone's relationship stopped there, we would pity that person. We would say that he or she hasn't really lived. Existed maybe, but not really lived. Why? Because that person has not experienced relationship with other humans. To borrow a business term, there is 'value added' by these human relationships.

"Furthermore, Chad, as a believer, I can tell you that you haven't lived completely until you have added the value of a spiritual dimension to your life, a personal relationship with God. In fact, I no longer have to tell you that, because you have experienced that relationship. For the first time in all your years, you are living, completely."

"Doc, this spiritual dimension, as you refer to it, really is a new discovery for me. It's like I've known about God, but until now, there has been no relationship. Not that I understand all there is to know about the relationship."

"Of course you don't, Chad. Neither do you understand all there is to know about your relationship with your physical environment, or your relationship with me, for that matter."

"That reminds me, Doc. I've hesitated to ask this question until now. But, just why are you spending so much time with a guy like me? I'm certainly not 'adding value' to your life."

"Oh, you're wrong there, Chad. You are adding value to my life. You see, we now have a mutual interest which serves to deepen our relationship. You have challenged me to express my faith in the simplest of terms, without using all those churchy words that most believers rely upon."

Doc continued, "You and I have not known each other long. But, because each of us has been willing to be vulnerable, our relationship has matured very rapidly. I told you about the problems of alcohol in my life. You have shared with me the emptiness you felt and allowed me to be a part of your search for a spiritual dimension to life. Our relationship would never have clicked if one of us had not chosen to make ourselves vulnerable.

"The same is true of our relationship with God. You do

realize that we could never have a personal relationship with God if God had not chosen to become vulnerable? Christians understand that God chose to become man, in the personality of Jesus Christ, just so it would be possible for humankind to know him as we know each other. God became vulnerable in Jesus Christ. Christ risked rejection, even to the point of suffering physical death, so that a personal relationship between man and God would be possible. That's how believers understand that Christ died for us. Remember our discussions about sin?"

"Yes," I responded quickly, "sin is missing God's goal for our lives."

"Right, and a part of this goal is for man to develop a true relationship with God. When we fail to develop that relationship, we sin against God. But when we are willing to become vulnerable to this force which we cannot fathom, then we have made our contribution to a personal relationship with God. A new relationship is born. There is new life because there is a new relationship."

"But what I don't understand, Doc, is what God is getting out of this relationship."

"Well, you've got me there, Chad. The wisest of men have puzzled over that question. They could only answer with a question of their own, 'Who can know the mind of God?'. Yours is a fair question, however, and it deserves a better answer than I have given you. Here is how I have come to terms with the question. I call it spiritual geography."

At that moment, Batty approached with the burgers we had ordered. "Great timing, Batty. We were just in-between lessons," I said.

"Enjoy," he replied, probably sensing the serious tone of our discussion. He left without further comment.

Doc removed the top part of the bun on his burger and played with the toppings until he found the huge slice of raw onion.

"Doc, what is it with you and onions?" I asked.

He chuckled. "Teachers need to be resourceful. I'm setting up for my next lesson. Chad, you eat, I'll talk. Batty's food is always too hot for me anyway," Doc said. I obliged.

Doc separated the onion slice and chose the two largest rings. He laid them on the table so that the circles partially overlapped.

"Explanation," Doc began to teach again. "I've already said that God chose to visit man in the person of Jesus Christ so that man could have a personal relationship with God. This is a graphic representation of that. Christ often referred to the earth as a collection of kingdoms. He used the term 'kingdoms of this world' to refer to the realm of human activity on this earth. Let's let this slightly smaller ring represent that world.

"In contrast, Christ began his teaching by proclaiming that the 'Kingdom of Heaven is at hand'." Doc lifted the larger onion ring and moved it toward me. Now, Chad, if I told you that something was at hand, what would that mean to you?

"That it was close enough for me to touch or pick up," I guessed.

"Exactly. Chad, I always thought it strange that most folks pictured Heaven as 'pie in the sky in the bye and bye.' Christ preached that it was something available to be grasped immediately. That's why I made the circles overlap," he said, replacing the Heaven onion to its original position. "You're going to love this," he said. "Lift a couple of the pickles off my burger, Chad."

"Are you kidding, Doc?" I looked around to see who might be watching. Seeing no one, I plucked the only pickle I could find off the top of Doc's burger. Then, I peeped inside my own burger and slid out another pickle. "Now what?" I asked.

"Place one of the pickles inside the world, but outside the overlap with Heaven. Then, put the other one inside the overlap." I followed Doc's instructions.

Doc continued, "Christ's mission was to introduce to man the possibility of becoming a part of a 'kingdom' that intersects our physical world, yet extends far beyond what our senses, intellect and emotions can fathom. Chad, did you ever decide to become a part of something which you did not comprehend completely?"

"Sure, Doc. I came to college, didn't I?"

"Ahh...right." Doc considered my response carefully to see if it provided an appropriate analogy. "You are a senior and you now understand college a lot better than you did when you entered as a freshman. And you have benefitted greatly from being a part of the University even though you will never completely grasp all that is here."

"I get the picture. While this new Kingdom of Heaven is available to me now," I said, fingering the pickle inside the overlap, "there is a large part of Heaven which I cannot understand because it extends beyond the borders of my physical world." My finger traced that part of the heavenly onion which did not overlap the world.

"Exactly, Chad. However little we understand about this kingdom called Heaven, some of us are willing to become a part of it now because we can perceive the possibilities. We perceive that God desires much more for us than we can now understand. But, to understand and function in this new kingdom requires something beyond our natural instincts, senses, intellect and emotions. It requires syncing our spirit with the Spirit of God. God's Spirit, which we call the Holy Spirit, is our link with the Kingdom of Heaven. If the docking has taken place, we find ourselves with a sort of dual citizenship. We are citizens of this world and citizens of God's kingdom." Doc outlined each onion ring as he spoke. Then, his finger found the pickle I had placed outside the overlap. "If we choose not to dock our spirit with God's, we have only our own faculties to sustain us.

"Let me do one more thing to our illustration, Chad." With the skill of a surgeon, the blind man meticulously lifted away the onion ring that represented the physical world, leaving the pickle that was formerly inside the overlapping rings now encompassed only by the circle representing the Kingdom of Heaven. Even more striking was the other pickle, now stripped of any relationship to either world.

"Chad, let this burn into your consciousness. It is a picture of eternal life and death. Your decision to allow God's spirit into your life will serve you well in this world, but it will be indispensable when all your other relationships are severed."

Doc's silence was intentional. I closed my eyes with the rapidity of a camera lens, hoping to imprint my last visual image permanently upon my memory.

Doc broke the silence. "All these circles have made me hungry. Pass me the catsup."

"But wait, Doc, you still haven't answered my original question. What is God getting out of this personal relationship with me?"

"Oh," Doc reacted with surprise. "I did promise to speculate about that, didn't I? Let me ask you a question then. I've defined one onion ring as the 'world' and the other as the 'Kingdom of Heaven.' You tell me what the overlapping area should be called."

"Well, Doc, I guess it's the Kingdom of Heaven on earth. But, does it have another name?"

"Yes, we call it the church." Doc answered. "Surprised?"

"Yeah, I know what the church is, but I would never describe it in those words."

"Think about it, Chad. You probably can't quote a lot of Scripture, but can you recite the Lord's Prayer?"

"Sure," I answered. "Our Father, which art in Heaven, hallowed be thy name. Thy kingdom come, Thy will be done on earth as it is in Heaven."

"Stop right there, Chad. Do you realize what you just said? This is a prayer that Jesus was teaching his disciples to pray to God. He was expressing God's desire that the Kingdom of Heaven should be a reality on earth. The implication is that the heavenly kingdom would completely and perfectly overlay the earth so that the life that exists in Heaven would exist on earth." Doc fumbled with the two onion rings until he got the larger one to completely overlap the slightly smaller one.

"Chad, I believe that God wants more than to simply live in you and me. As wonderful as that reality is for us, God's plan is larger than us. You see, I believe God's purpose is not just to dwell in man, but to dwell among all men. By occupying individuals who are vulnerable and willing to allow the Holy Spirit to penetrate their lives, God's presence can truly dwell among us. These individual lives form conduits through which God's presence can pass into the world. This way, the community of believers called the church can provide a dwelling place for God among men. And, I believe God intends that this community of believers should be expanded until it encompasses the whole of mankind.

"Chad, I know you felt the presence of God the other night at the hut. You felt it because the men there, Batty and Tom, have learned to allow God's spirit to flow through them. You were surrounded by a small community of believers, a small part of the church."

"I understand what you're saying, Doc. I did have an awesome feeling being a part of that group at the hut. But, you can't really believe that the church as we know it is anything like the one you just described."

"No, I'm not that naïve. But I do believe that God intends His church to be that kind of community. Unfortunately, the institutional church has missed God's intended purpose for it. By definition, the church itself sins and the world mocks its hypocrisy. However, I do believe that there will always be a community of true believers among whom God is pleased to dwell. You have experienced the benefit of being a part of that community. This is the Church to which we must be committed.

"Now will you let me eat my burger?" Doc begged.

"Okay," I answered, "but there's a lot I still don't understand about this Kingdom of Heaven, or about my spirit, or about this Holy Spirit. And what about my moral inventory? You told me you could introduce me to someone who could help me."

"Tom Morehead is the man you need to see," Doc answered. You remember Tom from the hut. He's leaving town later this week for some big economic conference in Rome, but I'm going to call him later and ask him to give you a lesson in spiritual economics before he leaves. He'll call you about the arrangements. Now you talk while I eat this cold burger. I need to hear more about this other relationship in your life, this Callie girl." Doc finally took his first bite of hamburger.

"What is there to say? It's a relationship that's going nowhere. Doc, I may be a novice in spiritual matters, but I'm good with the women. At least, I thought I was…until Callie."

Doc spoke with his mouth full. "Unfortunately, I don't have a lesson on romance, Chad. I'm afraid you are on your own with that relationship. I'll tell you what, though, Tom's spiritual economics lesson might help."

"Doc, what does spiritual economics have to do with Callie and me?"

Doc paused to wash down the bite of burger with a gulp of Cheerwine. "Oh, I don't know, Chad. Would you have ever thought that spiritual anatomy and spiritual geography had anything to do with onion rings?"

Expectation Management

Dear Callie,

You have no sane reason to take this note seriously, but I beg you to give me one last chance. Callie, I'm a different person, different even from the guy you talked to Sunday afternoon. There is a great movie playing at the Valley Mall Cinema. Please meet me out front Friday at 8:45.

Chad

P.S. If this sounds like the act of a desperate man, that's just what it is.

So, what else could I do? Callie won't even return my calls. I wrote her this note and drove by her dorm on the way to Tom's place. I spotted a girl that lives on Callie's hall, called her over to the car and told her to give the note to Callie. Why do I feel like I'm in the third grade again?

Tom Morehead's house at 312 Elm Street is not where I would live if I were a successful business consultant. It's a nice enough house, a ranch style, probably 20 years old, with some cosmetic changes designed to bring it into the modern era. Looks very cozy, but not at all "successful." Doc Masters set up this appointment and told me not to be late because Tom had to leave for Rome this very afternoon.

Tom's wife met me at the front door. She's just as I imagined, pleasant smile, neatly dressed, as though she were going out. A sort of older version of a 1960's TV mom.

"Come on in. Tom's in his study, Chad," she began. "He's told me what a fine fellow you are. I know the two of you will enjoy your conversation. Here, take this tray with you. I just took these cookies out of the oven."

"Thanks, Mrs. Morehead, you didn't need to go to this trouble," I responded, while balancing the tray and the Bible Doc had insisted that I bring.

"Hi, Chad," Tom said, as I entered his study.

It was clear that Tom was prepared for my visit. There was a portable chalkboard standing at the ready between two semi-comfortable-looking chairs. The room's walls were lined floor to ceiling with books. A small desk rested in one corner. There was no phone. In fact, there were none of the trappings of the business tycoon I was led to believe I was visiting.

"You brought your Bible, I see," he remarked.

"Yes, sir, Mr. Morehead. I have a brand new copy right here."

"Chad, remember my name is Tom."

"Right! Tom," I confirmed. "I know your time is valuable. Should I sit here?"

"That's fine, Chad." Tom pulled the other chair closer to mine. "I know this may feel strange to you, but I want us to have a prayer together."

You bet it felt strange, but what *didn't* feel strange these days. I watched Tom for my cue. He closed his eyes and lowered his head. I copied him. He began, "Father, will you please reveal to Chad the truth which you have shown me?"

Enough silence elapsed that I perceived Tom had ended what I thought must have been the world's shortest prayer. "Wow," I said without thinking, "you get right to the point Tom. This truth must be pretty important to you."

"You bet it is, Chad. It's the most important lesson God has ever taught me. And, the fact is, I cannot teach it to you. I can tell you what I know, but you will never learn this lesson unless God teaches it to you through the Holy Spirit."

At that moment, I had the urge to interject a question about this Holy Spirit, but I thought better of it.

"I don't want to bore you with my life's story, Chad," Tom continued, "but you need to know how I came to understand this mysterious truth. Tom rose from his chair and began to pace slowly around the room as he told his story.

"I was just a few years past college when I got my spiritual economics lesson from the school of hard knocks. I had a Master's degree in Business, a loving wife, an infant daughter and a fine administrative job at a community college near here. We attended church regularly and were active in community affairs. My life's plan was way ahead of schedule.

"My father had founded an office supply store in a small town nearby. The store grew quite rapidly. So rapidly that Dad had taken on other investors and some bank debt in order to expand. The pressures of the business became so great that Dad developed health problems—emotional problems, actually.

"Having the business training and feeling some family obligation, I offered to quit my job and join the business. I have to confess that my motives were not totally honorable. Honestly, I thought this was my big chance to strike it rich. What made me think that, I do not know, because my father surely had not gotten rich. But then, he wasn't an M.B.A. either.

"The plan was for Dad to be the front man, handling public relations and heading the sales force. I was to be Mr. Inside, managing accounting, purchasing, inventory and so forth. A great plan, but…Dad's health proved to be too far gone. He had to quit the business altogether.

"All of a sudden, Mr. Inside was Mr. Outside, Mr. Everything. I was frozen with fear. I hadn't bargained for this. I was petrified of selling. I was on the advanced slope and I hadn't even completed the beginner's course.

"Conditions went from bad to worse. We were losing sales, we were losing customers, we were losing big money and the bank was losing patience. Finally, I decided the problem was larger than I could handle. I began to call on God. After all, hadn't I been faithful all those years? Surely, I had the right to call in some of my spiritual coupons.

"My prayers went something like this: 'God, you know what my problem is. We just need a little help. That big order we bid on yesterday, if we can get that, I think I can handle it from there. God just get us past this loan payment. Then, somehow, I'll find a way to make this thing work.'

"I had gotten my wife in on the praying by this time. But the more we prayed, the more desperate the situation became. I would go into work at 5:00 am and work until late at night. Then, I would begin to pray. From morning until night I carried around this huge lump in my throat.

"One night, I found myself kneeling beside my easy chair in the den. I began with the same bargaining prayer. Then, the hopelessness of the situation overwhelmed me. I blurted out my resignation. 'Alright, God, you win. I give up.'

"The shocking response was swift and I will always believe God's words were audible. 'Well, it's about time, Tom. Let's see if you can do it my way this time.' Words cannot describe how

I felt as the weights of hopelessness and fear were instantly lifted from me. I know this sounds trite, but it felt literally like a
rebirth, as though the pressures of the womb had given way to
freedom of fresh air in my lungs. It was like a sign that God was
giving me a new start on life. I went to the bedroom to awaken
my wife and tell her what had happened. She was sitting up in
bed. She had just had an experience identical to mine. As we
compared notes, we agreed that we would do whatever was necessary to untangle ourselves from the business, even if it meant
starting over financially.

"It did mean starting over. I resigned my position as general
manager of the store, which bought some time until the store
could be sold. All the investors took a financial bath and I was a
failure in business. I found myself approaching my former em-
ployer about the very same teaching position I had held straight
out of college ten years earlier. I got the job teaching first-year
business and economics courses at the community college. It was
really like starting over. From that fateful night when I surrendered my will, my prayer has been that God would teach me
how to live.

"Chad, take your Bible and find the Old Testament book
called Isaiah." I started to fumble through pages that had never
been turned before. Tom reached over and parted the pages at
just the right place. He smiled and said, "Find the 55th chapter
and read verses 8 and 9 out loud."

I flipped a few more pages, ran my finger down to verse 9 and
began. *"My thoughts,"* says the Lord, *"are not like yours, and my
ways are different from yours. As high as the heavens are above the
earth, so high are my ways and thoughts above yours."*

Tom let the words soak in, then he spoke. "In view of my
business failure, it was easy for me to admit that God's ways
must be different from mine and that they were higher and better

than mine. But what I wanted more than anything was to understand those ways and to make them my own. As I read further
in the Isaiah passage, it became clear that God's ways could really be grasped. Look further down the page, Chad. Do you see
where God says that the word would not return void?"

I moved my finger down the lines of print, stopping at that
very verse.

"So, I reasoned," Tom continued, "if I studied God's word,
the Bible, with the same diligence I pursued my academic disci-
pline, I might find some clues. There is no doubt that I learned
plenty during the next few weeks, all very valuable. But, frankly,
I had the sense that I was just hovering around the truth, but
never grasping it. One night, I reread this Isaiah passage and the
truth leaped out at me. I was still using my own intellect, trying
to discover truth that must be on a higher plane. I needed help
to reach that higher plane.

"It was a few days later that I ran into Doc Masters. Literally,
I did. I had been in the University library to pick up some books
to use in teaching Economics 101. Hurrying out the library door
I rammed this guy and the books went flying. 'Can't you see
where you're going?' I yelled indignantly.

"'No, I can't, can you?' the question came in reply from the
ground below. It was delivered in such a tone that I was instantly
disarmed. 'Well, aren't you going to help an old blind man on his
feet?' my victim added.

"Of course, when I realized that I had just decked a blind
guy, I fell all over myself to make amends. I must have asked him
a dozen times if he was hurt. I finally got him over to a bench
near the library steps. We both sat. I drew a deep breath.

"'Well, can you?' the guy asked me.

"'Can I what?' I asked.

"'Can you see?' I will never forget the way he uttered those words. It was as if this blind man could see not only everything about me, but everything inside me.

"'Why are you asking me that question?' I asked, not really thinking that I had just asked the blind man the same question.

"He answered, 'Well, you were obviously preoccupied with some very heavy thoughts. Not really watching where you were going. A wise lady once told me that if I couldn't see out, maybe I should try looking within. Why don't you try that advice?'

"'What makes you think I need her advice or yours?'

"'I don't know, it just seems that you are distracted, possibly searching for something which is beyond your sight.'

"'Sir,' I replied, shaking my head in amazement, 'I don't know you from Adam, but I think you might know more about me than I know about myself. Could I buy you a cup of coffee?'

"We introduced ourselves as we walked a couple of blocks, his hand lightly on my left elbow. We found a corner booth in the campus snack bar. Chad, I'll bet you can guess what he ordered."

"Cheerwine," was my one-word answer.

Tom and I enjoyed an understanding chuckle. Then, Tom continued. "Doc and I made small talk for a minute or two and laughed about the collision. Soon we fell silent. I stared straight into Doc's eyes. I knew those eyes didn't function for him, yet they were piercing me to the very quick. I broke the silence. 'Doc, do you believe in fate?'

"'I believe in God. Is that the same thing?' he asked.

"'Maybe,' I said. Then I began to tell this total stranger my story, the one I've just told you. He listened intently, bobbing his head occasionally to signal his continuing interest. When I had brought the story line up to the moment, I paused to receive the blind man's insight. He used both hands to rub his unseeing eyes, put his hands on top of his thighs and leaned toward me.

"'Do you like hamburgers?' he asked me.

"I was glad that he couldn't see the disappointment on my face. I was expecting mystical insight, and he was thinking food.

"I had not perceived that darkness has encroached. 'Ahh, yeah,' I replied, stretching out the words, while I thought about my wife's dinner waiting for me at home.

"Doc yelled across the snack bar, 'Batty, are you there?'

"The man behind the counter yelled back, 'You know I am, Doc. And I know what you want. What about your friend?'

"Wait a minute, Tom," I interrupted, "was this the Batty we know?"

"Is there any other? Can you believe that I met both of my closest friends for the first time that day?"

"Now that really *is* fate," I observed.

Tom continued with his story. "Anyway, we ate hamburgers and drank Cheerwine while Doc told me the story of his physical blindness and his spiritual awakening. My problems paled in comparison, but Doc never made light of them. Instead, he lectured me on spiritual biology and talked with me about how God uses the Holy Spirit to make His ways known to believers. He reminded me that Jesus had said our job was not to worry about the affairs of this life, but to seek first the Kingdom of God. Then, he said, all the other answers would fall into place.

"Doc encouraged me to treat God's Spirit as a real person, the unseen friend that Jesus had said he would leave for us. He cautioned that it would seem strange at first, and he did not recommend conversing with the Spirit in public. But, he said that as I grew more comfortable with the friendship, the answers I was seeking would come. Heavy stuff, huh, Chad?"

I rolled my eyes.

"I know. I felt the same way," Tom reacted to my gesture, "But you'll learn just as I did."

Tom continued his story. "It was pretty late when we exchanged addresses and phone numbers. Doc formally introduced me to Batty and invited me to join the two of them for a late-night get together which I later discovered was the weekly S.O.B. meeting. Batty explained that midnight was the only time he had for a meeting. He worked two jobs, this one as a soda jerk from 5 until 11 and his day job on the University's maintenance staff. I politely declined the invitation. I knew I was in enough hot water with my wife because of this little escapade.

"As I was leaving, Doc called to me, 'Tom, wait, you're about to forget the very book you came to the library to get.' I checked the stack of economics textbooks in my arms and glanced at the booth we had occupied. I had indeed left one of the books.

"Batty picked the book up, gave it a quick inspection and tossed it on top of my stack. 'That old Doc's got pretty good eyesight for a blind man, doesn't he, Tom?'

"That's an understatement," I said as the door closed behind me.

"Driving home, I marveled at the strange events of that afternoon and evening. Call it fate, call it what you will, I knew that I could not pass this experience off as mere coincidence. So, right there in my Buick, I spoke to God's Spirit as if he were a real person. It was a one-sided conversation, but I told 'the Holy Spirit of my desire to know the ways of God and of my frustrating search of the Scriptures for answers. I confessed my earlier conclusion that the answers must lie on some higher plane than my own intellect and that unless I could get some 'supernatural' help, my quest would only end in frustration.

"There was silence. I heard no reply. What came to mind, instead, was Doc Masters' advice to me. 'If you can't see out, look in.' The thought no longer seemed the useless contradiction it had earlier. Then, Jesus' words about seeking first the Kingdom of God and His right ways came to mind. It occurred to me that I had been looking for God's ways from my own human perspective. Maybe the direction of my looking was backwards. What if it were possible to view man's ways from God's perspective? That would mean seeing myself through God's eyes, not God through mine. I remember wondering, could, *would* this Holy Spirit provide such eyesight?

"I also remember wondering, as I tried to find the keyhole to our back door, if this Holy Spirit ever intervened in domestic matters. It was very late, all the house lights were off, my wife was in bed and I was in the doghouse. I crept into our bedroom, library books still in hand, and planted a soft kiss on Dorothy's cheek.

"'Honey, I'm sorry I didn't call. I was over at the University and…'

"'Can we have this conversation in the morning?' her sleepy, but firm voice interrupted. Without further conversation, I re-submitted my kiss and crept out of the room.

"I plopped the library books on my study desk. The one on top slid off, making a rather loud noise. I grabbed it quickly as if I could somehow silence the noise. As I picked it up, the parting conversation in the snack bar came to mind. Doc had said that this economics textbook was the one I had come to the library to find. What could he have meant?

"I opened the book and thumbed the first few pages. There on page four was a diagram explaining man's motivation for working. Pure, basic, unquestioned capitalism, Chad."

Tom paused. He walked over to one of the bookshelves that lined the room and returned with a rather dog-eared copy of an economics textbook.

"Chad, Doc told me you're a senior."

"That's right," I answered. "Is that important?"

"Well, yes. It means that the first part of this lesson will be review for you."

"I wouldn't be so sure," I hedged. "I took Econ as a freshman."

Just like a professor, Tom ignored my editorial comment. "Okay, Chad, describe what is represented by this diagram." He handed me the book, opened to page four. I stared at the diagram.

"Oh," I surprised both of us. "I do remember something like this. Here you have a horizontal line indicating a person's expectations and a parallel line below it representing his resources or abilities to meet those expectations. And, this gap between the two lines they call the *satisfaction gap*. It's called that because all of an individual's economic expectations cannot be satisfied if he doesn't have adequate resources."

"Hey, you're pretty good. Did you ever think of becoming an economist?"

"Are you kidding? This is the only chart I understood all semester!"

"Well then, you know that the explanation is that man will work to raise his resources so that they are in equilibrium with his expectations. At that point, there would no longer be a satisfaction gap. His expectations would be fulfilled."

"But," I said, feeling smarter all the time, "the example points out that man is a creature of consumption. As his resources begin to close the satisfaction gap, he inevitably raises his expectations. It's the good old capitalist's way."

"And the result is…" Tom prompted.

"He must work even harder?"

"Yes, and…"

"Man is never satisfied. His expectations always outpace his resources."

"You bet! That's man's way. Most good capitalists would even swear that it is God's way. Chad, this is the very page I saw that night. Right there, I tried an experiment. I did as Doc had instructed. I acknowledged that God's Spirit was in that room and that the Spirit was like a real person with whom I could converse. The conversation was not audible, but it went something like this: Okay, this diagram represents man's basic thinking about why he is motivated to do work. Is this the same rule you use in your kingdom?

"Chad, you'll find that the problem in conversing with God's Spirit is that you seldom hear a voice. It is more like the thought is translated to you. Then, it is up to you to put it into human words. As I waited for the Spirit to speak, a radical thought entered my mind. Jesus had made a comment that John recorded in his gospel. Here, trade books." Tom exchanged the Econ textbook for the Bible. "Find John, Chapter Ten."

I had less trouble with this one since it was the book Doc had recommended that I read. "What verses?"

"The last part of verse ten, I think," Tom answered.

I read, "I have come that you might have life and that you might have it more abundantly."

"Chad, the thought I had was that in God's Kingdom there would be abundant life; that is, plenty for everyone. Enough that there would be no satisfaction gap. But how?

Chad, I'll offer you another tip. When you are dealing with God's Spirit, you can almost always take man's thinking and turn it 180 degrees. Can you discover another way to close the satisfaction gap?"

"180 degrees, huh," I stalled for time. Then, the inspiration came. "Yeah, sure, the guy could just lower his expectations down to the level of his resources."

"Bingo!" Tom shouted.

"But that's not the American way," I protested.

"Precisely, but it is God's way."

"Well, haven't you just burst the capitalist's bubble with one fell swoop?"

"Not really, Chad. In fact, this concept is the salvation of capitalism. It adds what capitalism lacks; it makes it whole."

At that moment Mrs. Morehead opened the door slowly. "Dear, don't forget the time. Your airplane will not wait and you promised to run that errand for me."

"Oh, okay, Dorothy, we'll finish here shortly," Tom responded.

"Chad, I really do have to speed this up a bit. We can have that conversation about capitalism some other time. But for now, let me just leave you with some food for thought that may be more closely related to why you are here.

"What I discovered that night was that this principle of expectations was applicable, not just to economics, but to every area of life. Take personal relationships for instance. Marriages, to be specific. Chad, why do you think there are so many failed marriages today?

"I don't know. Folks just can't always agree, I guess." I knew it was a stupid answer, but at least it was an answer.

Tom continued the quiz, "Think about it in terms of the expectation chart, Chad." I revisited the Econ book. The light came on. I went straight for the chalk board and began to draw and talk simultaneously.

"Why sure, Tom, look here. If you let the bottom line represent one spouse's resources and the top line represent the other spouse's expectations, they'll always have problems as long as there is no equilibrium. And, if the Econ example holds, as soon as one mate's resources begin to approach the other's expectations, those expectations rise and create new dissatisfaction."

"Did you ever think of becoming a psychologist, Chad?" Tom grinned.

I continued my discourse. "Well, it's so simple. If the couple wants to be content, all they have to do is lower their expectations of each other. The lines will converge and they will be satisfied with each other."

"Well, Chad, you know that life, especially when it's concerned with personal relationships, is not that simple. It is not always best to lower our expectations of others. What we must do constantly is to take inventory of our expectations. Then, with the Holy Spirit's help, we can settle on the appropriate level of those expectations. From that point on, it becomes God's problem. Remember the Scripture, seek first the 'rightness' of God and all these things will be added to you. That is to say that if we have agreed with God upon a level of expectation, God promises to raise the level of resources to meet those legitimate expectations. Just think of the marital misery that could be avoided if couples practiced just a little 'expectation management.'

"Chad, you'll be amazed at the applications of this little truth. Take my advice. Don't let this lesson elude you. Think about it, pray about it, until it becomes a tool for daily living. If you make that happen, you'll begin to live the abundant life about which Jesus spoke. Chad, pray one more time with me.

"Father," Tom prayed, "please make your Holy Spirit Chad's friend and teach him Your ways. Thank you, Father."

There was really no need for further conversation, but politeness demanded it. "Thanks, Tom. I know this meeting was inconvenient for you. I hope your flight to Rome will be a good one. When will you be back in town?" I asked.

"I'll miss the next S.O.B.'s meeting, but I'll see you next week. Here, stuff a few of these cookies in your pocket. We don't want Dorothy to think her cookies didn't come up to our expectations."

Pop-top Romance

For the first time ever, I felt conspicuous driving my red convertible away from Tom's place. My life has been one big expectation. Somehow this car seems to symbolize my inability to find satisfaction. None of the new toys I have acquired has ever really narrowed the satisfaction gap in my life. The abundance of things has really failed to provide me with the abundant life. And I am the culprit.

For the first time ever, I drove to the University library with true excitement about the prospect of finding something there which would change my life. I paused a moment at the bottom of the library steps. My mind replayed the violent meeting of Tom Morehead and Doc Masters, and I couldn't help but whisper a prayer of thanksgiving for those two men. In a matter of days, they and Batty had fed me more of the meat of life than I had gleaned from all the books in this library. Now, I was in search of one book that had obviously made a difference for them. It wasn't the Bible...I had that in my hand. It wasn't that economics textbook which had meant so much to Tom. No, what I wanted to find was the book from which the S.O.B.'s had taken their society pledge. All I really knew about it was that it was used by Alcoholics Anonymous.

With that scant bit of information, I was able to find a copy. Like many of the volumes in this library, the internal pages had never been touched by human hands. The pages were hard to part. While this particular copy had not been touched, I was sure that millions of copies had been read and heeded. The little book did, in fact, contain the twelve steps which had helped so many people overcome alcoholism.

It was easy to do as the S.O.B.'s had done. I simply substituted the word "sin" for the word "alcohol." After all, alcoholism is just an example of one way we miss God's goal for our lives. The word "sin" is generic. I reviewed steps one through three.

"We admitted that we were powerless over alcohol [sin] and that our lives had become unmanageable."

"We have come to believe that a Power greater than ourselves can restore us to sanity."

"We have made a decision to turn our lives over to the care of God as we understand Him."

I drew a deep breath. It was amazing how these steps traced the road I had traveled these past few days. However, it was step four that had occupied my mind since I first heard it at the Society meeting.

"We made a searching and fearless moral inventory of ourselves."

How do you take a moral inventory? What do you count? What values do you assign to the inventory list? Who's to keep me from cheating? I shut my eyes to mull over these self-posed questions. My mind's eye saw page four of the Econ text. There was the graph, the resources, the expectations, the satisfaction gap. I remembered Tom's words about how God's ways and man's ways differ.

Man's way of inventorying is to count and value his assets,

his resources, I thought. Then, God's way must be to evaluate one's expectations. Yes!

Making a searching and fearful moral inventory means examining my expectations, not my resources. It is at the point of my expectations that my morality is rightly or wrongly established. Not only that, but now I know the source of the objectivity I need. It's the Holy Spirit.

Step five sealed the deal.

"We admitted to God, to ourselves, and to another human being the exact nature of our wrongs."

Well, Holy Spirit, I know you are not human, but you *are* a being, so I guess you and I had better get acquainted. There is a lot of work to be done and very little time to do it.

That last thought had a blasphemous ring to it. But I understood the guys to say that God overcame that mystical barrier between man, first in the form of Jesus Christ and later by the Holy Spirit. If the Holy Spirit is going to be the personal counselor, teacher and helper that Jesus said he would be, then it only seems right that we should be on a first-name basis. No disrespect intended.

Painful, yet cleansing. That's how I would describe the sleepless night I spent in my apartment with the Holy Spirit. I emerged from it exhausted, but freed; condemned, but pardoned; humbled, yet exhilarated. It turned out that the expectation inventory was only the beginning. Steps six and seven of the A.A. Twelve Steps Plan required that I humbly ask God to remove my shortcomings, i.e., adjust my expectations. Step eight required that I make a list of all the persons that my misguided expectations had harmed. I had to become willing to make amends to them all.

That list was a long one. At the top of it were my parents. My

God, how I have used them over the years to satisfy my own selfish expectations. Step nine required that I *"make amends to those I had harmed, wherever possible, except when to do so would injure them or others."* I determined to have my parents' names stricken from my list very soon. The others would take more time. But there was one which could not wait. I had to set things right with Callie. I asked the Holy Spirit to use whatever influence he had upon her to give me the opportunity I needed. What's a small favor like that among friends?

꙱

I stood in the chilly night air in front of the mall cinema, shoulder to shoulder with hundreds of others waiting for a chance to get inside to the warmth, if not the movie. I knew that this was something of a showdown for Callie and me. I'm not sure I thought she would show up. But I had to keep my end of the bargain. So I waited.

Several times I rolled Tom's abundant life theory over in my mind. Okay, God, I confessed, maybe I have focused my energies on Callie's inability, or unwillingness, to meet my expectations. I'm a red-blooded American boy. Are my desires unreasonable?

I had already learned that neither God, or His Holy Spirit, were great conversationalists. All I got were those words of Jesus, "Seek first the Kingdom of God and His right way." Did this mean that I should forget about Callie altogether? Should I just concentrate on the lessons I had been learning as a new believer? Would I really be willing to do that, to give Callie up for the Kingdom of God? For his righteousness?

I found myself praying, "God, if this is your answer, just don't let her show up."

"Hey, Chad, you lucky guy," came a call from the street in front of the theater. It was one of Callie's crazy friends hanging out the car window. From the far side rear door popped Callie. It was just like one of those slow motion movie scenes where everything becomes fuzzy but the beautiful smiling girl, who moves radiantly toward her lover.

"Well, did you think I wasn't going to make it?" she smiled.

"Ahh…" I stalled to give myself time to awaken from my dream. "Ahh…no, no, I knew you'd be here. You cut it awfully close. I'll bet the movie has already started."

"Chad," she said, "I don't want to see the movie. Let's go for a drive."

I could tell that she had plotted her strategy. Callie was going to have her say once and for all. "Okay," I agreed. "I've seen this movie anyway."

Small talk would not come to either of us. We sat side-by-side in my Corvette. Before I turned the ignition key, I decided to throw her off balance. I looked straight into her beautiful eyes and said, "Callie, have you ever done something truly spontaneous?"

She paused, and with a little smile, she reached into her purse. She pulled out a toothbrush, waved it in my face and said, "Well, it's not exactly spontaneous, but it is new for me."

Now it doesn't take a rocket scientist to take a hint like that! I could only mumble, "But the girls…"

"They aren't expecting me back tonight, Chad."

My head sunk to the steering wheel. I was the one who was off balance. This can't be real. Here is my greatest expectation served up on a silver platter. *Why me, God?* I muttered under my breath? I knew this was the moment of truth. Doc, Tom and Batty had been teaching the lessons, but now Callie was administering the exam.

"Chad, are you all right?" Callie's anxious voice revived me.

"Oh, of course. Let's go," I said, turning the key and revving the engine. "Callie, this calls for a celebration. I'm going to take you to the most special place in all the world."

"Chad, can't we just go to your apartment? This isn't the easiest decision I've ever made, you know."

"No, absolutely not. This will be like heaven." I got the Corvette into cruising speed and offered my hand to her in comfort. She accepted.

"Chad, we're headed out into the country, do you think it's safe?"

Then I uttered those famous words, "Trust me, Callie, trust me." We moved along Route 12 until we came to the small dirt road and the clearing near Doc's hut. I stopped the car and went around to Callie's door. "We have to go through a little bit of woods here, Callie." She said nothing, just got out and grasped my hand tighter than ever. Her hand was damp and cold.

"Here, put this blanket around you," I urged. I had grabbed the blanket from behind the seat where it stayed for just such emergencies. She accepted it, wrapping it over her shoulders and grabbing my hand once more.

Callie followed my lead down the one-person path. My flashlight revealed the hut at the end of the path. Moving around to the pond side, I flashed the light over the top of the door. "Watch your head," I said.

"S.O.B.," Callie asked, "why in the world is that there?"

"So you won't bump your head, silly," I teased her.

Inside there were the makings of a fire. Doc was always careful to be prepared for his next visit. Callie spread the blanket on the dirt floor as I got the fire going.

"Isn't this just the greatest place?" I asked.

"Well, I hadn't pictured things being like this, but I guess there is a certain romance about it," She answered. We lay silently together, listening to the fire crackle.

"Chad," Callie broke the silence. "I never, *ever* thought that I would give myself to anyone before marriage. I just wasn't raised that way. But I'm afraid of losing you. I don't know why. Sometimes I don't even like you. But I need you, Chad. I love you."

We embraced. I could have stayed in her arms forever. But this hoax had gone far enough.

"Callie," I said, breaking the embrace. "I'm not the guy you think I am. I told you in my note that I've changed. It's true. The thing I've always wanted from our relationship is no longer my primary desire. All this time I have tried to reach you on a physical level and now that it's happened, I know it's not right. Not now."

In the flickering light Callie's face looked puzzled, but obviously relieved. "We never hit it off intellectually," I continued. "You were always reciting the straight and narrow. I never saw the serious side of life. That is, until I met Doc Masters." I propped myself up on one elbow. "Callie, I just discovered tonight that what we have transcends the physical and the intellectual. Our relationship is spiritual."

Callie had to be in shock by now. From the verge of surrendering her virginity, she was hearing her playboy lover speak of spiritual things. Yes, Callie, there is a God!

I spent the next hour, two hours I guess, telling Callie my story, from my acquaintance with Doc Masters, to the hut, to his lessons on spiritual biology and spiritual geography. I showed her Doc's chalk drawings on the wall. Then I picked up a broken piece of chalk near Doc's drawings and made one of my own. It was the overlapping circles. Inside the overlap, I drew two stick figures.

I told Callie about Tom and his spiritual economics lesson. I told her how God had changed my expectations of her that very night. Tears flowed down her cheeks. She could not speak.

Then, I did the most spontaneous thing I had ever done in my life. Glistening by the flickering fire was an "old-style" pop-top. I picked it up without attracting Callie's attention and worked off the tongue with my fingers. I grasped Callie's left hand which was trying to wipe some of the tears from her eyes. I slid the pop-top over her ring finger, kissed the tears from her eyes and asked, "Will you marry me?"

You cannot imagine the suspense that welled up in me as I gazed into Callie's eyes. The best I could really hope for was a "Let me think about it." The worst was a solid "No." Neither came.

What came was a smile of contentment and a soft, sweet "Yes." I don't know if it qualified by Tom's definition but that moment I began to experience the abundant life. I had taken God at his word and he had honored it beyond my comprehension.

Callie and I saw the sun rise over the mill pond that morning. We had talked the dark away discussing our faith, our hopes, our marriage and our future together.

Down by the water's edge was a quaint little boat. Though it had weathered in the elements, its name was neatly lettered on the stern, "*The Ark*." We wondered if *The Ark*'s owner would object if we borrowed it. No, we agreed, not for this special moment.

Golden leaves floated atop the still waters. *The Ark* slipped across the pond with effortless ease. Only its wake gave any hint of motion. If I had ever been in a more heavenly setting, I could not remember it. Neither could Callie. Looking back toward the hut, Callie observed its quaintness. I observed much more.

It was the temple of my faith. It would always be for me the Wailing Wall, the Mecca, the Holy City. It is where I found God, or perhaps where God found me.

Route 12

Callie and I spent Saturday together. She didn't want to go back to her dorm to face her curious girlfriends. I was tired, but afraid to catch even the shortest nap, fearing that I would awake to find last night had been a dream.

The two of us agreed that, at least for the next few days, we would tell no one about our marriage plans. Callie put the Cheerwine engagement ring on the gold necklace she wore. The contrast was comical and, in a way, symbolic.

It's amazing how little is required to entertain two people in love. We ate and we talked. We talked and we walked. We sat and we stared. By late afternoon, we were exhausted, wonderfully exhausted. As night fell, I did take Callie back to the dorm. What tale she told, I do not know. Me, I never made it as far as my bedroom. The living room couch accommodated me nicely.

Sunday, we went to church. Love really is filled with irony. The centerpiece of our former difficulties had been my unwillingness to go to church with Callie. Now we sat, hand in hand, in the balcony of the First United Methodist Church.

The scene resurrected all my old doubts about the church. Hypocrisy has always been my problem. Not my own, of course. But the hypocrisy of the smug, holier-than-thou church people surrounding me. I could never reconcile what I saw of them on Sunday with their lives the other six days of the week.

Before, the solution was simple. I would let them do their little religious thing as long as they left me alone. They obliged. Except for Callie.

Now, however, the gauntlet had been dropped. I was a believer, a citizen of the Kingdom of God on earth, a part of the church. But are these people surrounding me "the church?" And if they are, why don't I feel any kinship? These sounded like good questions for Doc. Anyway, I liked the music.

❧

I had called Doc Masters on Monday to ask if I could bring a guest to the Society meeting Tuesday night. He said that would be fine. Tom wasn't going to be back from his trip to Rome. There would be plenty of room.

Callie and I agreed during the drive out Route 12 that we would let Doc and Batty in on our news. They would keep our secret until we got home that weekend to tell our parents. After that, we would make the news public.

Doc and Batty were more than just a little surprised that my guest was female. They were speechless when I told them that she was my fiancée. I could see their surprise turn to joy as I told them the details of our spiritual romance.

"This calls for a celebration, Batty," Doc spoke up. "Break out the wine." Callie flashed her pop-top engagement ring as Batty passed out the Cheerwine cans.

After a while, Doc made sure the talk got serious. He asked Batty to lead us through the S.O.B.'s pledge. Batty pulled the old copy of the A.A.'s twelve steps from the crack in the wall where it stayed between meeting. He moved through the steps rapidly. Just as I had been, Callie seemed fascinated by the appropriateness of each step and by the sincerity of these men.

Batty finished with step twelve, *Having had a spiritual awakening as a result of these steps, we tried to carry this message to 'sinners,' and to practice these principles in all our affairs.* There was a prolonged sweet silence.

I broke the quiet, "Fellas, I want to thank you for taking step twelve seriously. I mean it! You two and Tom have changed my life."

"You're kind to say that, Chad," Doc replied for the both of them. "Of course, it is the 'truth' you have discovered that has changed you, not those of us who may have helped you to see it."

"And," Batty jumped in, "besides, you better not forget that you've just seen the road map, you ain't traveled the road yet."

"Batty is so right, Chad," Doc added. "Do you remember one of our early conversations? You kept asking why on Monday mornings you couldn't tell the Christians from everyone else."

"Strange that you should raise that point, Doc," I replied. "The fact is, excepting this group of S.O.B.'s, I still have a problem with that." Callie snickered at my abbreviated reference to the Society members. "There are thousands of people who do not know what the inside of a church looks like who are just as good as most of those church folks."

"Wait a minute, Chad, that's not fair," Callie interrupted. "Who are these thousands of 'good' people who never go to church?"

"Well," I began, "I was thinking about the people around us every day, but I guess you could make that millions and include those good people in other cultures. Are they doomed to hell because they don't know Jesus Christ?" I turned my question from Callie toward Doc with a glance in his direction, which of course he could not see.

"Doc, the boy is asking you," Batty said with a slight grin.

Doc gathered his thoughts. "We have to be careful here because we are really mixing two questions, neither of which is simple. In fact, this is pretty heavy stuff, but let me give it a shot. Let's take the question about people of other cultures or other faiths. The real question you are asking is whether they can know God without knowing Christ. Right? Let me illustrate your question with a mathematical equation."

Doc fumbled in his coat pocket for a piece of chalk while Batty rearranged his seat toward the side of the hut that Doc had used previously as a chalk board. It was clear that Batty, too, was interested in this lesson. Doc gestured toward a space on the wall which he thought was clear. Callie moved his hand a little to the right and gave him the okay.

"All right," Doc began, "Batty, quote us that Scripture passage from the book of John that folks use to prove that Jesus is the only way to God.

Batty paused just a second, "That would be the one where Jesus says 'I am the way, the truth and the life. No one comes to the Father but by me.'"

"Exactly, Batty, good job," Doc said. Now, let's do a little spiritual mathematics. We will put that statement in algebraic terms." He began to write a formula along one of the horizontal boards.

$$C = W (T \times L) = F = G$$

"Who can explain this equation?"

Callie spoke up. "I'll try. C is for Christ which equals the way, W, times truth, T, times L, life, equals F, Father, equals, G, God.

"You've got it, Callie! Do you think this equation fairly describes what Jesus was saying?"

Doc's three students looked at each other. "Yeah," I answered for the group.

"And, does it address your question, Chad?" Doc asked.

"Well, it will if the equation holds true."

Doc continued, "Let's see. There is no problem with the C for Christ, the F for the Father, or the G for God. But allow me to further define the terms in the center portion of the equation. W is simple. It stands for way. Remember, what we are trying to prove is that there is only one way to God. So, let's replace the variable W with a 1. Seems fair doesn't it? Then what about truth? Wouldn't you agree that it is a constant. I mean, truth should be truth for any time and any culture, don't you think? We all agreed.

"Then," Doc continued. "That leaves us to deal with the L, life. Can we further define life?"

"Yes," I answered. "You've taught me that life is defined as relationship."

"Correct, Chad," Doc acknowledged. "So, let's substitute the term R for relationship in place of the L. Now, how does the equation read?"

"Let me try," Callie asked. I could see that she was really into this spiritual math. She took the chalk from Doc's hand and wrote:

$$C = 1T \times R = F = G$$

"Christ equals one times the truth, times relationship equals the Father, equals God. If we multiply the middle portion of the equation, we get truth times relationship...we get a relationship with the truth!"

Doc coached her. "Yes, Callie. Go on."

She did. "If we have a relationship with the truth, we will

know the Father and Christ. They are equal, they are the same. They are God!"

"How about that!" Doc said with some satisfaction, putting his chalk back in his pocket.

"That's neat," I admitted, "but what does it prove?"

It was Batty's turn. "Well, I think what it says is that if a person of any culture can develop a personal relationship with the truth, he can know God. But the key would be some kind of ongoing relationship with the truth. That's not easy. How do you have, not just a knowledge of the truth, but a relationship with the truth?"

"I can help you there, Batty," Doc said. "These kids won't remember, but you might. Do you remember when Jesus was preparing to leave this earth? He said that he would send someone to take his place."

"The Holy Spirit," Batty answered.

Doc was still coaching. "Yes, but he gave that spirit another name. Remember, Spirit of ..."

"Truth," Batty answered quickly. "Yeah, the Spirit of Truth. And that's the truth with which we really can have a personal relationship."

"But," Callie questioned, "do we have to know about Jesus to have this personal relationship with the Spirit of Truth?"

"The operative word here, Callie, is 'know,'" Doc said. "You see, Christians believe that God the Father, the Holy Spirit, this Spirit of Truth, and Christ are one. If you have a relationship with one, you have a relationship with all three.

"There may be many ways of learning about the truth, but truly only one way to have an ongoing relationship with it. In other words, the routes to this relationship may begin from many different locations, but the journey is the same. It is an inward journey that every individual must take, one step at a time.

As a Society of Believers, we believe there are twelve of those steps.

"Anyone who comes to know the Spirit of Truth will know Christ, regardless of the name he is called. Likewise, anyone who has a continuing relationship with the Truth will know God the Father. It is simply impossible to know one without knowing all three.

"Now that we have solved this spiritual equation, let me explain why the S.O.B.'s are followers of Christ. Chad, if your heart's desire was to get to Crystal Lake, how would you set out to get there?"

"I would first ask for directions," I said.

"And, who would you ask?" Doc continued.

"I would try to find someone who had been there. That person would be my safest bet," I said.

Doc continued the quiz. "But how would you know for sure if that person had ever been there?"

"Well, in the final analysis, I guess I would just have to trust someone who assured me he had been there," I acknowledged.

"What if I told you that Route 12 would take you there? Route 12 is not the greatest of roads. In fact, it is very narrow and it is not well-traveled. But I am sure it will get you there. Remember now, Chad, your heart's desire is to get to Crystal Lake. What are you going to do?"

My answer was quick. "Oh, I would trust you, Doc."

"Why?" he asked.

"Because I believe you've been there," I said.

"Chad, Callie, that's exactly why I trust that Jesus Christ is the best way to God. I acknowledge that there may be some other routes to God, but why would I take another route when someone I trust has been there and says 'follow me'?"

It took us a moment to let this latest spiritual lesson sink in.

In fact, I was glad when Batty called for a recess of the S.O.B.'s meeting and invited us to join him for a good stretch and the fresh air outside the hut. The night was cold but clear. The moon that had been full just a few nights earlier was now waning. Still, its reflection on Thurston's mill pond brought my mind back to the night Doc and I had first met at the hut. And, to that night of nights when my world turned around—that night when Callie said she would be my wife.

Callie broke the spell. "Let's go back inside, Chad, I'm cold." I took the opportunity to wrap my arm around her and to usher her inside.

When we all got back inside, Doc resumed the conversation. "I haven't forgotten the other part of your question, Chad. You were puzzled that the people you see around you every day seem altogether as 'good' as those folks you sat next to in the pew last Sunday. That bothers you, does it? Tell me again what you said earlier about there being thousands of people…"

"Yes," I said. "There are thousands of people who never go to church, who are just as good as the ones who do," I explained.

Doc came back. "Ah, you just put your finger squarely on the problem, Chad. You make the mistake all non-believers and most believers make. You assume that the distinguishing quality of a believer is goodness. Correct me if I'm wrong, but you think that the central struggle we all face in this world is between good and evil. Am I right?"

"Sure," I answered.

"Even I believe that and I've been a believer longer than Chad," Callie added. "At least, I thought I was a believer."

"'Course you are," Batty said reassuringly. "Like Doc says, most believers think that way."

"And because they think that way," Doc continued, "goodness and evil, especially goodness, is the yardstick by which believers are measured and by which they wrongly measure others. Callie, would you agree that goodness can be learned?"

"Well, yes, I suppose so. Our laws are supposedly good. We learn to accept them as good and act accordingly."

"Good example. Now, is it not true that even criminals can learn and do good; that is, obey laws, when it fits their own purposes?"

"Yes, they can be good, but their goodness is selective, on their own terms," I added.

"Precisely," Doc agreed. "It follows, then, that believers, too, can learn and practice goodness. And, since the world views this goodness as the measure of their faith, it behooves believers to act especially good at times."

"Chad, would you also agree that human goodness is a relative term, being defined differently by different individuals or different groups?"

"Yes," I answered. "There is common agreement on some goodness, but much of it is subjective."

"And," it was Callie's turn, "a lot of it is situational."

"I suppose you mean that man's definition of goodness can change with the circumstances?" Batty asked. "that it is possible to do good as we understand it and still, say, hurt others?" Callie gave an affirmative nod.

"These kids are sharp tonight, aren't they Batty?"

"Yeah, Doc, go ahead, give 'em the punch line."

"Kids, what Batty and I are trying to get you to see is that most believers, even though they may have once had an experience of grace, think they are required to learn and act out goodness by themselves. Chad, do you remember when we had you act like you were leaning on an imaginary post?"

I jumped to my feet and assumed the awkward position. "Hey, Callie, I'll bet you can't do this!" I challenged.

She made no attempt to join me, but she said, "I could for a while, I imagine. But no one has the strength to do it for very long."

"But while you are leaning, it can look very convincing," Batty observed. I began to wobble a bit from the strain and gave up the pose.

"And when you fall..." Doc picked up my train of thought.

"...you look very human," I finished.

"That's right. It's a sort of 'Catch 22'," Callie had caught on. "Most people's measure of Christians is 'their' personal goodness. Christians, in order to be judged good, expend their own energies learning and acting good. Situations arise when their judgment is poor or their strength is just not equal to the challenge. Their learned goodness is exposed. So, non-believers are left to conclude that Christians are just actors."

"Hypocrites," I added.

"You couldn't be more correct," Doc agreed. "one of the reasons Christianity is so misunderstood is that Christians have led the world to believe that the central struggle in life is for goodness. We've discovered that life's central struggle is not for goodness, but for wholeness."

Obviously, neither Callie nor I could disguise the puzzled looks on our faces. Doc knew more explanation was in order.

"Callie, did Chad tell you that I am a recovering alcoholic?" Callie looked at me, silently seeking permission to confirm that I had told her about Doc. My smile was sufficient.

"Yes," she replied, "but he also told me lots of good..."

Doc interrupted her, "I have long since learned that consuming excessive amounts of alcohol is not good. As a matter of fact, I knew that even while I was drinking heavily. So, why do you suppose I kept on drinking, even though I knew it was not good?"

"Obviously, you couldn't help yourself," Callie answered.

"Right, but why couldn't I help myself?" Doc countered.

"That, I don't really know. It seems that some people have that weakness," Callie replied.

"Then, it is a natural thing?"

"Yes, for some people," Callie continued.

"Callie, I'm a biologist. I'm convinced that my alcohol weakness is very natural. One day, this alcohol weakness will probably be traced to a defective gene. I understand that there was a set of social circumstances that caused the weakness to surface. But what I want you to see is that my problem is not really a matter of choosing to do good or evil, it is a matter of a deficiency in my natural self.

"Chad can tell you the details of my awakening to the truth about my condition. The key was the discovery of the Twelve Steps. As I read them, I saw that they were not just another goody-goody approach to my problem. They formed a very scientific approach to my natural weakness. The steps helped to reveal an understanding of the problem, provided insight into the remedy, and gave me a set of activities designed to replace my natural weakness with wholeness.

"As I acknowledged my natural weakness, God supplied a supernatural power, which I now know as grace. That grace has allowed me to overcome the weakness. The weakness is still present, but it is overpowered by God's grace.

"It didn't take long for me to recognize that the weakness for alcohol was not the only natural shortcoming in my life. Nor did it take a rocket scientist to figure out that when I admitted my shortcomings and invited God's help, the grace to overcome was always there. These successes convinced me that the Twelve Steps are a prescription for wholeness. And the natural, or I should say the supernatural, by-product of that wholeness is goodness, but not my own."

"So," I chimed in, "to sum it up, believers should concentrate their energies on being whole and the goodness will follow as a nat...*super*natural consequence of the wholeness."

"Well, that's the gist of it," Batty spoke up. "But here is another reason why you have a hard time distinguishing Christians from everyone else. The Twelve Steps are a prescription for wholeness. But most Christians don't realize that all sin, like alcoholism, is a chronic disease.

Doc picked up the thought there. "In order to stay on the wagon, every day I live I have to confess that I am an alcoholic. A recovering alcoholic, but an alcoholic nonetheless. To convince myself that I was cured would be to invite disaster."

"Right," Batty jumped back in. "And since alcoholism is just one form of missing God's goal for us, the same is true of all sin. Recovery from sin is a process we call salvation. But most Christians understand salvation as a cure. Once they feel healthy, they take things in their own hands again. After all, the Bible says, 'God helps those who help themselves'."

"Of course, you know that the Bible says no such thing," Doc corrected Batty, giving him a wink of assurance that they both knew the truth. "What it really says is that man's strength is deep within himself at the level of the spirit. That is where he is to live his life.

"Ironically, the most difficult time to make this principle work is when things are going well. This is precisely when our self-motivation is strongest. The Scriptures say that 'pride goeth before the fall.' Pride is nothing but self-interest taking the driver's seat. When it happens, we are blinded to our continuing need for grace. In that blindness, we falter."

"Doc, are you saying that believers are most vulnerable at the point that they feel most righteous?" I asked.

"Without question, Chad," Doc replied. "That's why you have always viewed believers as hypocrites."

"That's scary," I reacted. "But how can a new believer like myself prevent that from happening?"

Doc stared at Batty. Batty returned the stare. There was a silence I did not like.

Doc transferred his stare to me. He looked like a judge about to pronounce a sentence. "Chad, the lesson that every true believer has to learn sooner or later is that…"

"Hold it, Doc," Batty broke in. "I know what you're going to say and I have the perfect illustration. It's like one of your spiritual lessons."

Doc stopped. "Okay, Batty, let's have it," he said.

"Oh no, not here. This lesson is for another day." Batty turned toward me. "Chad, ask Callie if you two can take a field trip with me on Thursday. You do have to get permission, don't you?" he asked with a wide smile.

Callie smiled back. "That comes after the marriage, Batty. Sure we can come, can't we Chad?" I nodded my head in reluctant agreement.

"Good. I'll call you guys with the details tomorrow," Batty said.

"Hey, what about me," Doc pleaded. "Don't I get to come along?"

"Absolutely not," Batty came back in feigned seriousness. "You blind people always want to tag along. I'll take you some other time."

Doc poked out his bottom lip. "Well, if that's the way it's going to be, I'm going home. Batty, do you want to drive or shall I?"

Batty jumped to his feet. "By all means, allow *me*."

The Fountain

The arrangements were for Tom Morehead, who was just back from Rome, to drive by for Callie and me on Thursday. Batty was bringing the tools in his old pickup. We were to meet him at the mysterious destination around 4:00 pm.

Tom's Buick pulled up in front of my apartment at exactly 3:30 on Thursday. That Buick mirrored Tom's style: It had some age on it, but it was spotlessly maintained. Maybe it was because Doc had told me how financially successful Tom was that I was so keenly aware of Tom's frugality. Most men would wear such frugality as a cloak of humility. It was more deeply and comfortably woven into Tom's basic fabric.

Callie hopped into the front seat. I got into the back and immediately thrust myself forward between the two of them to make the formal introduction. Tom beat me to it. "You are Callie, of course. I'm Tom Morehead, one of the three S.O.B.'s that Chad knows."

Callie chuckled. "Proud to meet you. Chad has told me about you and about the time you spent with him last week. You should know that the things you shared with him really changed his life and mine, right, Chad?"

"Yeah, Tom. Things really began to click for me after our time together. I even asked Callie to marry me," I added.

"I know all about it," Tom confessed. "Batty and Doc both relayed all the details. Seriously, congratulations to the both of you! Hey, we had better start motoring if we're going to get to the church on time."

"The church?" Callie and I questioned in two-part harmony.

Tom started the Buick. "We're going to Batty's new church on Downtown Boulevard. You don't know the background on all of this, do you? Let me catch you up as we go. Let's see, where should I begin? You probably didn't know that the church where Batty is a member lost its building to a fire a few years ago. Chad, you've seen all that remains of it in that opening just before you take the woods path to the S.O.B. hut."

"Oh," I reacted. "I never knew that was a church. Callie, you may not recall seeing it. All that is left is the old stone foundation, the steps and a few charred timbers."

Tom picked up the story. "Unfortunately, the small congregation had no insurance and so they were left without a place to worship. Batty, Doc and I were meeting occasionally at the campus grill where Batty still works. After we had consoled Batty, Doc told him that his church's misfortune could be just the break Doc had been looking for. Doc said something like, 'I've always wanted a little place out from town.' Doc said his parents had left him a piece of land on the Downtown Boulevard where his dad's old business had been. The old buildings had been torn down and it would make a great site for a new church building. Doc asked Batty if he thought his congregation might be interested in an even swap.

"It was all I could do to keep my mouth shut," Tom continued. "That proposal was just about like swapping the Plaza Hotel for a landfill in New Jersey. That piece of property on the boulevard was worth a small fortune and Doc knew it. Batty highly suspected it himself."

"'You crazy man. What kind of fool would make a deal like that?' Batty asked Doc.

"Doc stared me right in the eye, mentally daring me to take issue with him...ahh, Tom is my tax man. He knows that the swap would give me a really good tax break.

"Batty looked at me. I shrugged as if to say, who am I to dispute my client?

"To make a long story short, I did help Batty's church and Doc negotiate the world's most one-sided trade. After that transaction, the church was able to sell part of its new property to the State Bank and use the money to get themselves well along in a building program. When I shared this story with a contractor friend and a couple of guys in the building supply business, they made the church offers that couldn't be refused. Within a year, Batty's congregation was worshipping in the new facility. Isn't that a great story?"

"It really is," Callie responded. "Was it really a tax break for Doc?"

Tom chuckled, "Doc uses that old line about a tax break all the time. Doc Masters has given away everything he ever owned and that includes all his current income except for his modest apartment rent and food money. A six-pack of Cheerwine occasionally is his only luxury. He always reminds me that my tax advice has saved him thousands of dollars. Sure, if you give it all away, taxes are not a problem."

Tom pulled his Buick into the parking lot of State Bank. "It works out perfectly to have all this parking near the church. On nights and weekends, the bank is happy to share it," he said.

Turning off the engine, Tom paused with both hands on the wheel, took a deep breath, as if to gather his thoughts. Then he turned and placed his right arm on the back of his seat so that he could face Callie and me. "The two of you are most fortunate to have met Doc Masters at this particular time in your young lives. Chad, you've told me that you consider Doc to be the happiest person you have ever known. I probably know more people than you do simply because of my age. My travels have allowed me to meet people all over the world. I know people with uncounted wealth, people in the depths of poverty, famous people, people of all faiths and religions, old people, youngsters. None of them have Doc's consistent exuberance for life. It goes beyond contentment. It's as if there's a wellspring of peace and joy, not just filling him, but overflowing him onto and into the lives of others.

"For years, Batty and I have asked ourselves what it is about Doc that's different from any other human being we know. We now think we know. It was Batty's idea to have you two watch him put the finishing touches on a project to honor Doc. We think it will not only honor the man, but it will testify to his secret of successful living. Just let Batty do his thing and then all of us can literally sort out the pieces together."

Tom turned and opened his car door. Callie and I stared at each other in delighted puzzlement. When you're around these S.O.B.'s, you begin to expect the unusual. We hopped out of the Buick and followed behind Tom as he lead us toward the quaint little brick church sitting back from the busy boulevard. It was surrounded by young pine trees, which provided a barrier to the business of life nearby.

"The church had always been known as Piney Grove Church," Tom said, still walking toward the building. "They had to bring the pine grove with them when they moved to town."

Piney Grove Church. That name rang a bell with me, but for the life of me I couldn't make a connection.

Now we were on a brick walkway that led around to a courtyard formed by the pines and the inside angle of the L-shaped building. As we turned the corner, Tom stopped. There was Batty, seated on a wooden bench gazing at a large granite object that stood in the center of the court. It appeared to be a fountain of some kind. A circular pool held a large cup, perhaps six-feet high. Actually it looked like a polished granite chalice. There was no water. Apparently this would be the first time the fountain would be turned on. A sort of christening of a huge christening font.

The sound of our movement stirred Batty from his contemplation. "Where have you been?" he asked. The gleam on his face belied his feigned anger. "I'm ready to get on with this. Tom, did you tell them what we are up to?"

"Well, yes, in general terms, Batty. But maybe you'd better do the explaining," Tom replied.

"Oh, okay." Batty was clearly pleased to be asked to emcee this ceremony. "Here, you two sit right here." He pointed to the bench which he had recently occupied. Callie and I took our seats front row and center. I folded my arms and nodded my head toward Batty to acknowledge our readiness for the curtain to rise.

Batty began, "Now let me pick up where we left off the other night at the hut. Doc was about to tell you what every true believer has to learn sooner or later, right?" We nodded simultaneously in agreement. "Remember that we talked about learning to be good, how most Christians think this is their primary duty. So, they're continuously polishing their lives like this cup here." He pointed toward the centerpiece of the fountain. "They scrub and polish so that others can admire their shiny finish."

Batty motioned Tom toward the building, moving his hand in much the same way a maestro would beckon his orchestra to prepare to receive his downbeat. Tom opened an inconspicuous door to a small room and flipped an electrical switch. The almost inaudible hum of a motor, obviously the water pump, echoed our way. We waited, expecting to see a burst of water spraying from the chalice. Or at least a stream cascading over the lip of the cup. Nothing happened.

"Is something wrong, Batty?" Callie whispered.

"No, child. Everything is just right," Batty assured us. By now we could see enough water lapping over the cup's edge so that it darkened the granite. But only a few drops fell into the pool below. Obviously, the pump had just enough pressure to fill the cup, but not enough to push the water over its lip.

"That's just right. She works just like we planned it." Batty's comment was directed to Tom who was making his way behind Callie and me. Tom nodded.

"You see, children," Batty resumed his lecture, "there's a second group of Christians who believe God wants to fill their lives from within with grace. So they don't concentrate so much on how they look to others. Their emphasis is to be filled with God's goodness. They study the Bible, they pray for the Holy Spirit's presence, they encourage each other in their efforts. However, they never seem to be filled and only occasionally does this cup full of grace ever spill out to the benefit of others."

Then Batty fell silent. Standing between his audience and the work of art, he rubbed his hand across his mouth and chin, contemplating his next move. Whatever image we may have mentally formed of that next move was soon shattered—literally shattered.

"You know, Tom," Batty said, raising his voice, "this thing is just not complete. There's still work to be done here." Tom said nothing.

Batty pulled a sizable chisel from his rear pocket and retrieved a small mall-hammer from its resting place underneath one of the pines. He walked toward the fountain. Tools in hand, he stepped up onto the granite side of the pool. It was a stretch for Batty to place the chisel on the lip of the chalice facing us. My chin began to drop uncontrollably as my mind processed the scene. Hammer met chisel with one huge blow. Pieces of granite flew. Water gushed over Batty and then began to fill the pool below. Batty had created a permanent crack in the granite. Now the water found its way freely out of the cup. The splashing sound brought a coolness to the autumn air. What had appeared to be an act of destruction had become an act of release.

Now the steady flow of water from the crack led my eyes downward to words inscribed on top of the granite retaining wall of the pool. Callie, too, had noticed the inscription. We rose from our seats together, as if on cue, and walked to the pool. I stood while Callie bent down, and following the words around the circular pool, she spoke them aloud.

"The water I give him will become in him a spring of water welling up to eternal life. John 4:14"

Callie paused momentarily, as if acknowledging the break between words, and then continued reading the inscription.

"Through the cracks of personal desire flow the waters of passion that nourish the fields of true contentment. Jeremiah C. Masters."

Callie eased herself to a sitting position on the side of the pool. She fingered Doc's last few words with eyes closed as if, somehow, the Braille reading would sink more deeply into her being.

Glancing up, I saw that the frail black man was in tears. A huge white arm wrapped around his neck, drawing his head to a broad chest.

My mind raced into the future. People will come here to escape from the busy boulevard. And without reading the inscription, regret that some vandal has marred a work of art. A child will splash the clear waters on his face and point to words saying,

'Read to me, mommy, read to me.' And the young mother will read the words in baby rhythm, not really understanding them herself. But some will come and the sight of art and words will unite head and heart. Suddenly they will decipher the ancient hieroglyphic communication within their own spirits. They will know even as I know this very moment. And they, too, will weep for joy.

Batty gathered himself. For a moment, I thought he was going to deliver an explanation for his destructive actions. He thought better of it.

"We didn't invite you here to lollygag around," Batty's now composed voice rang out. "We need to get a drape in place for Sunday's dedication."

"We really could use a hand from the two of you," Tom added. "Come with me." He led us inside a storage room, pointing Callie to a pile of plastic pipe and me to one end of a long roll of canvas.

With the materials on site, Batty talked us through the assembly process, which was obviously of his own design. It did the job. The canvas, supported by the pipe, soon surrounded the fountain. Batty dusted off his "unsoiled" hands, signaling that the job was complete.

I policed a few stray bits of broken granite, depositing all but one in a trash can as we walked toward our vehicles.

Batty put one foot up on the running board of his truck, ready to explain all that had transpired at Piney Grove today. "I hope you children understand why Tom and I had to do this. We know that Doc doesn't personally need or want any honoring. But, we just needed to say thank you, don't you know?"

"Well, we appreciate your letting us be a part of this act of love," I said, fumbling for words of significance. "If it weren't for

Doc, Callie and I wouldn't be traveling home this weekend to tell our parents about our wedding plans."

"Oh no!" Tom's reaction surprised us. "Does this mean that you can't be here Sunday afternoon for the real dedication? Can you make it back by four o'clock?

Callie and I exchanged inquiring looks and reassuring nods. "Yeah," she answered for both of us. "We'll be here at 4:00 sharp. We only live a couple of hours away."

"Great!" Batty exclaimed. "Oh, and if you talk to Doc, don't let on about this. We want it to be a surprise." He turned and began the slow ascent into his pickup. Tom motioned us to the Buick.

Once we had safely merged into the rush-hour boulevard traffic, Tom spoke. "Chad, last week I told you about my own private lesson in expectation management. You remember how I had to learn the hard way to focus my spiritual attention on the level of my expectations and not simply concentrate my energies upon building my human resources."

"Yeah, Tom," I answered, "I used the graph from the text-book to explain it to Callie. That lesson was one of the things that made me realize how unreasonable my expectations of her had been. It was like Doc's quote on the fountain. When God shattered my personal desires, I saw Callie in a way I had never seen her before. Suddenly, she became more to me than I could ever desire. Strange, isn't it?"

"Not really," Tom replied. "Expectation management is most easily understood in financial terms, but I think its most useful application is in the arena of relationships. You know, Chad, I felt badly about rushing off to the airport last week. I felt I had left our lesson somewhat incomplete," Tom said.

"How so, Tom?" I asked.

"Well, I wanted you to understand two other things about expectation management that I didn't have time to make clear the other day. First, not all of our expectations need to be lowered. We must simply be willing to have them pass under the light of God's scrutiny. That exercise will dictate whether we lower our expectations or decide to trust God for adequate resources to match those expectations.

"Second, in circumstances where God has successfully adjusted our expectations, our resources will meet our expectations and provide the personal satisfaction we talked about the other day. But God's purpose goes beyond our personal satisfaction. Really, our satisfaction is just a by-product. God wants our resources to overflow our expectations. Then, those excess resources become available to assist others who need them to meet God's expectations in their own lives. Those overflowing resources represent God's love being poured out through us to our fellow man. Think about that. And let me remind you that these overflowing resources are not just financial. Think about those people you know who seem to overflow with emotional or intellectual or spiritual strengths that others need. That's love in its truest sense.

"But," Tom went on, "let me use another financial example, one from Batty's life, to illustrate these two points about expectation management. Sometime after my own learning experience, I shared my spiritual economics lesson with Doc and Batty. Doc was intrigued that I had discovered a tangible way to explain the philosophy he had tried to live out in his own life. That's when he first spoke those words you read on the fountain.

"Batty was not an immediate convert. He said to me, "Alright, smarty, answer me this. What do I tell my youngest daughter, Elaine, who is convinced that she can become a medical doctor? Do I just tell her to pray to God and he will lower her expectation level just like that? Or, should I just use God to break the news that our family can't afford for her to dream that big?'

Doc broke in. 'Batty, Tom isn't saying that every expectation we take to God is going to be automatically crushed. The idea is to allow God to weed out those desires that are selfishly motivated. If any of our dreams are God's dreams too, then it is God's responsibility to see that they become reality. So, yes, you tell Elaine to talk to God about her dream. Tell her to see if God thinks that becoming a doctor is a worthwhile ambition for her. And, if God does, tell her to go for it.'

"Then, Doc asked Batty what he thought of the dream. Batty said, 'I had a dream just like that when I was Elaine's age. It was not a question of wanting to be somebody, it really was a desire I had to serve others. But I faced two huge obstacles. I was dumb and poor.'" We all chuckled.

"'Fortunately, Elaine doesn't have the dumb problem. But the poor problem is big enough. The reality of poverty woke me up from my dream. In time, the same reality will wake Elaine up too. She won't need God's help for that.'"

Tom had reached my apartment by now. He pulled the Buick up next to my Corvette and unfastened his seat belt so that he could look directly at Callie and me. He continued his story. "So, Doc asked Batty if he knew what it meant to be passionate. Batty replied that it meant having strong feelings about something. Like a man might have for a woman he loved." I glanced at Callie, raising my eyebrows a la Groucho Marx.

"Doc made Batty look up the word passion in the dictionary. He got a surprise. Chad, what is your definition of passion?"

"I don't know, I like Batty's definition," I mumbled.

"Well, in fairness, the word has come to mean a strong desire or feeling. But its origin is quite different. Our word is derived from a Latin verb, *pati, p-a-t-i,* which means to suffer."

"Oh," Callie's light came on. "So it's like when we talk about the passion of Christ."

"Exactly, Callie," Tom continued. "Jesus said on more than one occasion in the Scriptures, 'I do nothing of myself. I do only what my Father tells me to do.' Do you see what he was saying? He constantly surrendered his personal expectations to his Father. But when he knew what his father really expected of him, he didn't let his apparent lack of resources stop him. He was willing to suffer, even die, to make it happen. That's passion!"

Tom hesitated, "I forgot to ask if you guys have time for all this talk," he confessed.

"Don't stop now, Tom," I insisted. "Finish Batty's story."

"Well, Doc told Batty the same thing I just told you about Christ's passion. Then he looked Batty straight in the eye, the way only that blind guy can, and said, 'I'm not sure Elaine is ready to be passionate about much of anything at her age, but I want to know if you are.'

"'I are what?' Batty came back.

"'Are you ready to be passionate about Elaine's dream to be a doctor?' Doc asked.

"'Why should I suffer for her silly dream?' Batty said, softening his tone with each word.

"'For the same reason Christ suffered for you, Batty, because his Father asked him to. It may be time for you to examine your own expectations in the light of Elaine's dream. You see, Batty, what God is trying to do in each of our lives is to get enough cracks in our cup of personal desire so that our overflowing resources will water the dreams of others. At that point, we simply become conduits of God's love. You will be amazed at the joy such living will bring.

"'But Batty, you need to know that there is a price to be paid for this lifestyle. That price is passion. Do you think you are capable of that passion?'

"'Listen to what you're telling me, Doc,' Batty replied. 'You say I've got to have passion, which you define as suffering. Then, you tell me this passion, this suffering, is going to lead to happiness. Doc, it just doesn't add up.'

"'Well, you've got me there, Batty. In man's plan for living, there's no room for suffering. There's no room for passion unless the personal rewards are great enough. And, it seems that God is patient to allow each of us to try man's plan. But God does offer a *Plan B*. That's spelled "*Be.*" And while it does not compute in man's rational mind, I can tell you that Plan "Be" works for those who will exercise the faith required to try it. I'm asking you, Batty, do you have the guts to try it?' Tom paused.

"I never saw a man clam up so quickly or so tightly. Batty literally did not utter another word to either of us. I told Doc later that I thought he had been too hard on Batty. We both thought we had lost a dear friend.

"It took Batty about two weeks before he would speak to either Doc or me about that conversation. When he finally did, he told us how he had wrestled with Doc's question. He said that he had never had any problem believing in God or understanding that God wanted to be an active part of his life. But Doc's challenge had hit him right between the eyes.

"He did talk to Elaine about her desire to become a medical doctor. He was convinced that she had the passion to make it, if she could be given the chance. He knew that it would mean tremendous sacrifice for his family. He also knew that the real decision rested upon his shoulders.

"Batty told us of a little book he had read years earlier. It was about a Welshman named Reese Howells. Howells was a Christian, but he felt that God was calling him to resign his job and take on a full-time prayer ministry with no pay. The book described how Howells came to the point when he felt God must have an answer. When it was apparent that he was not humanly capable of making the sacrifice, Howells heard God speak to him, *Reese, if you are not willing, are you at least willing to be made willing?*

"Batty had decided that he was willing to be made willing to follow Plan Be. At this point, that willingness had to be good enough. He had asked the University to switch his working hours in the snack bar to the second shift so that he could take classes at the community college. He thought he could get a better job, maybe even hold down two jobs. He and his wife, Nellie, would put their personal expectations on hold. They would suffer whatever was necessary to make Elaine's dream possible. In short, Batty had found the passion." Tom smiled. "Perhaps the two of you can meet Dr. Battle this Sunday. She will be coming to town for the fountain dedication.

Callie leaned over and gave Tom a kiss on his cheek. "That's a real *Reader's Digest* story, Tom," Callie said. "The message to a couple just starting out together is pretty clear."

"It's clear, all right, but that doesn't make it any easier," I added.

"It does make it easier in one respect," Tom added. "Both of you certainly have your own personal dreams and expectations, but you will need to merge them into one set of dreams. That will take surrender to each other and to God. But you are very fortunate. Even before you are married, the two of you can make the basic decision. Will you choose man's way or God's—Plan A or Plan Be?

We ended our conversation with some small talk about our trip home to tell our parents about our engagement. We assured

Tom that we would see him at four o'clock Sunday afternoon at Piney Grove.

I had to take Callie back to her dorm. I'm sure she thought nothing of the switch from Tom's old Buick to my Corvette. But the symbolism wasn't lost on me.

Good News

It was as if someone had beamed us home. The conversation with Callie consumed our time awareness. We found ourselves in Callie's parents' driveway.

I wasn't sure of the order of things. I had never consulted Emily Post on the subject of wedding announcements. The way I had it figured, there was no need to talk to my parents if Callie's folks nixed the whole idea. How will Callie's preacher-father react? He knows everyone in our town. He knows my family. Well that's probably a plus. But he knows me, at least he knows about me. He has probably lectured Callie about guys like me. "Now don't you go off to that university and take up with the likes of that Clayborn boy. You find yourself a solid, church-going fella that will settle down and love you." I could just hear him.

This was the first time it struck me that there were only a handful of people who knew that I had decided to turn my life around. Even my own parents had no clue. Everyone else only knew the old Chad Clayborn. Just because my past sin was forgiven, the consequences remained and they were staring me squarely in the face. But I was convinced that this marriage had God's blessing. "God," I whispered a silent prayer, "tell me this is not some stupid joke. This marriage seems so right. Please do for me what I cannot do for myself."

Callie was more confident of the outcome. She came around the car, opened my door, and dragged me out of the bucket seat by the arm. "Relax, Chad, he's not going to bite you." Biting was not what had entered my mind. Devouring was more like it.

Somehow we made it into the Simms kitchen. Her mother and father were finishing their after-dinner coffee. The two of us were holding sweaty hands. "Dad, Mom, this is Chad. You know his parents, the Clayborns, from the furniture store."

"Oh yes, Chad," Mrs. Simms rose from her seat. The Reverend Simms did not. "Thanks for bringing our Callie home," she replied.

"Our Callie." Here I am trying to find the words to ask if I can marry their daughter and she calls her "our Callie."

Just where I found the words, I will never know; they must have come right out of some romance novel, or better, straight from heaven. "It was my pleasure, Mrs. Simms. After these past few days, I can surely understand why you call her your Callie. In fact, that's really why I'm here. Reverend, Mrs. Simms, I want to ask if I can share your Callie. We want to be married."

There was a long pause. A very long pause. I mean, if this had been an intermission at the movies, everyone would have gone home by now.

"Well, Herb," Mrs. Simms said at last, "are you going to say something?"

"Aren't you the fella that drives that red sports car, that Corvette?" he asked.

"Ahh…, yes sir, I do. But I'm planning to sell it soon." This was news to me, too. It was as if I was having an 'out-of-body' experience. Could I be held accountable for this loose talk?

"Oh, too bad. I had just pictured you and our Callie making your get-away with cans tied to the bumper of that red thing," he chuckled.

"Ah, well, we could rethink the sale, but we will probably need the money. Oh, not that I won't be able to provide for Callie. Oh no, I have a couple of good job possibilities. I'm graduating this spring, you know. I don't know where we will live, but I'm sure it will be close by so that you can see Callie often. I..."

Thankfully, Callie snatched me from the grave I was rapidly digging. She left my side and leaned her head on her father's shoulder. "Daddy, this is the most important question you've ever been asked. Why are you making small talk about cars?"

"Well, actually I'm sure it wasn't small talk," I began to muddle. Callie's baby blues beamed a coded message my way. I deciphered it and clammed up again.

"You're right, darling," her father said. "I should be talking to you. Do you love this guy or has he brought you here under duress?"

"Oh, Daddy!" Callie replied with exasperation. "You always knew I would bring Mr. Right home someday. Today is that day. Chad is that man."

"Well, that settles it," the Reverend spoke the last word. "I guess I'll pronounce our Amen to that. Do you agree, Sarah?" Mrs. Simms spoke her agreement with open arms that drew Callie and me together. It was definitely a Kodak moment.

"So this is why you cooked four pork chips for supper, Sarah?" Reverend Dad observed. I gather you knew something which I did not."

"Chad," the Reverend addressed me, "I can see that the two of us need to have some lengthy conversations. I'm not sure you are prepared for this cunning twosome." He laid my plate on the table next to his own.

The dinner conversation dealt mainly with the plans. When was the big date? Was it to be a big wedding? Where would we set up housekeeping? I soon realized that this conversation was between Callie and her mom. The Reverend had detached himself from the gory details. My input was unnecessary. As the two women came up for air, the Reverend spoke, "Chad, why don't you and I take a stroll out back? The ladies seem to have this subject well in hand." He was right; those two hardly acknowledged our leaving.

The Simms house was a middle-aged red brick. It looked like a ranch from the front but the land sloped toward the back, fully exposing a basement and giving it a much larger presence. Most of the green was gone from the lawn. Only the heartiest of vegetables remained in the Reverend's well-tended fall garden. The impending darkness had thrown a damp blanket over the landscape. Our shoes accumulated the evidence.

The Reverend spoke. "Chad, let me be straightforward with you. Callie is our only daughter. Her mother and I have prayed her through these twenty-one years, with varying degrees of success. But there is one thing about which our prayers have been relentless. You are that one thing." We walked a while with only the sound of shoes parting the wet grass. He stopped. I halted on cue. His eyes met mine. "Son, I know more about you than I ever thought I would know about the boy Callie would bring home. And…well…that's what bothers me."

Of course, I knew what he meant. My playboy reputation had reached legendary proportions in town. My self-indulgent past lay squarely between me and the only thing for which I have truly had a passion, "our Callie." It was time to stand and fight, but with what? The Reverend had the truth on his side. He was wearing the white hat.

I looked down at the droplets on my loafers. My forehead felt equally dampened by a cold sweat. Then, I looked him in the eye. "Reverend, do you believe in God?" His nonverbal response turned my cold sweat to hot flashes. "Well, what I mean, sir, is that I do…believe in God, that is. And this is something new to me. It's new, but it has changed me. I cannot refute anything you've heard or believe about my past. I won't try to defend that. But that is the old Chad Clayborn. What you see standing before you is the new Chad. And, unfortunately, I have no evidence to support the change."

I stopped to collect my thoughts. At least I had the Reverend's attention. "I have no evidence, but I do have a witness. I just realized that Callie is the only person in the world that really knows both the old me and the new me. Reverend Simms, sir, do you know what it means to be passionate?"

"I know what most people mean when they talk about being passionate," he answered. "Frankly, that's what bothers me about all this, son. From what folks say, it seems you have a passion for being passionate."

"But, sir," I continued, "I mean real passion, like when you know that God has something for you and you are willing, even happy, to suffer for it…or for her. Sir, the only way I can describe the relationship Callie and I have is…heavenly! And, I mean that in the truest sense. It is a spiritual thing. I've never experienced anything like it. But, I am not willing to surrender it to my past. Loving Callie is the second most wonderful thing that has ever happened to me."

"And what might the first be, Son?" he asked softly.

"Finding God," I replied. "And to think, both of these wonderful discoveries have happened this week." Emotion now became my enemy. If my defense was not complete, it had nevertheless ended. The jury was out.

Now it was the Reverend's turn. A tear wove its way slowly over and down the wrinkles of his cheek. "Chad, all these year,

I have only prayed one prayer about the fella that Callie would choose for her husband. I prayed that I could call him brother, before I had to call him son."

His big hand extended toward me. I grasped it. He spoke the words of affirmation: "Brother, I'll be proud to have you as my son."

❦

There was none of the heart-thumping drama of that encounter with the Reverend when we went to my house. In fact, the second feature was more like a Broadway musical. Callie waltzed into the Clayborn household and stole the show.

As charming as Callie was, I knew that much of the euphoria of this moment was relief. Relief that the prodigal son had come home. Relief that his chosen one met all their criteria for a daughter-in-law: attractive, poised, well-bred, the whole shopping list. I was pleased. They deserved Callie.

Callie and my mom were instant friends. They soon made their way to the kitchen for wedding chit-chat. That left Dad and me in the den to have that father-son talk about responsibility. He wanted to know my plans for a job, a house, a savings account. All the while, I tried to find an opening to tell Dad about my spiritual journey. But I just couldn't.

Dad had lectured me before about these fundamental Christians and their religious quick fix. That's how he would see Doc Masters, Tom and Batty. It would be difficult for me to verbalize all I had learned. It would be like the two of us were on different radio frequencies. This evening was too important. I opted for safety. "Dad, tell me about how you and Mom started out." Just like that, Dad was in his glory.

Bad News

Driving back to school, Callie and I critiqued the weekend. Things went very well with the 'in-laws'. It was great fun breaking the news to our local buddies. We felt good. The homecoming seemed to have cast the die. We really were committed to follow through with this marriage thing.

Callie had already dressed for the dedication service. I needed a tie, so we stopped by my apartment before heading to Piney Grove. We were pressed for time, so Callie waited in the car while I rushed inside. My foot kicked a piece of paper that had been stuffed under the front door. I grabbed it on the run and threw it on my bed while I began my search for a tie.

Ties have never been a mainstay of my wardrobe. I had to rummage through my closet before I found one under my baseball glove. It was surprisingly well preserved and I even remembered how to tie the knot.

Breathing a sigh of relief, I took a moment to glance at the paper I had retrieved from under the door. It was a note from Tom Morehead.

Chad, I hope you read this message before you head for Piney Grove. There has been a change of plans. Batty and I will be at the hut. Meet us there. Bring Callie. We'll explain.

Callie didn't like my tie. She also did not like the sound of Tom's message. Frankly, I was puzzled, but decided to adopt a wait-and-see attitude. "Callie, they probably just told us the wrong time. Or, maybe they were going to…Oh, there's no use speculating. Let's just wait and find out what those two characters are up to this time."

The trip out Route 12 seemed interminably long. We finally reached the opening where the old Piney Grove Church had stood before the fire had reduced it to ashes. I pulled up beside Tom's Buick. I turned off the engine and was struck by the silence around us. Our conversation had long since ceased.

Callie and I tried to hold hands as we moved quickly down the one-person path to the hut. We could smell smoke, obviously coming from the hut. It was the kind of day that would not let smoke rise. The wind just filtered it through the trees.

The S.O.B. sign over the hut door became visible earlier than usual through the mostly-bare tree limbs. The same wind that carried the smoke had grounded a lot of the brown and wrinkled leaves which had been clinging to the branches for dear life. The wind and crackling leaves made the only sounds as we moved along the path.

Finally we reached the hut door. If this is some kind of gag, I'll let those two know what S.O.B. really means, I thought. Bowing our heads to clear the door, we caught sight of Tom and Batty, both seated in silence. No Doc.

Tom reacted off cue, as in a high school play when someone forgets his lines. "Thanks for coming. We were worried that you had missed my message and gone straight to Piney Grove. Did things go well this weekend?"

I wasn't interested in small talk. Callie did the honors. "Yes, very well, thank you. At least until we got your message. Is something wrong?"

Both men dropped their heads. "It's Doc, isn't it?" I said in reaction to their silence. "Is he sick?"

Batty's almost inaudible voice managed the words, "Doc passed last night."

"What? What do you mean, Batty?" I said, going to my knees to look him in the eyes.

Tom breathed deeply and reached for my shoulder. "Chad, Doc died about 3:30 this morning."

"Died!" I cried. "He was perfectly fine when we left him on Friday. Is this some kind of joke?"

"I'm afraid not, son," Tom answered.

Callie came to her knees and wrapped her arms around me from behind. Her moist tears ran down the back of my neck. She said nothing. Tom said nothing. Batty's labored breathing was all we could hear.

My chest burned. I've always been an emotional person, but at that moment there were no tears, only pain and bitterness. "This isn't really happening! How could God do this to a good man like Doc? Doc Masters, of all people!" I said in disgust.

"Now, boy, don't you talk like that," Batty stopped me. "Haven't you learned anything Doc taught you? You know God didn't take Doc's life from him. Sin killed Jeremiah Masters."

"What Batty means is," Tom explained, "Doc was shot."

"Shot!" Callie exclaimed. "You mean murdered?"

Tom shook his head in disbelief, "Well the police told us that a teenage boy broke into Doc's apartment in the middle of the night. They speculated that he was looking for money. Anyway, Doc must have awakened and walked in on the guy. He probably surprised the young kid. The kid fired three shots and then ran. One shot missed, but another caught Doc in the neck and the other one pierced his chest."

I held my hands tightly against my ears trying to press Tom's words from my consciousness. It didn't help.

Tom continued, "Neighbors heard the shots, but couldn't

111

find where they came from at first. By the time the rescue squad got on the scene, Doc had lost a lot of blood and didn't have a pulse. They revived him and rushed him to University Hospital. One of the nurses recognized Doc and called Batty because she knew they were friends. Batty and I got to the hospital just before Doc died."

I was mad at God. "I thought I had this religious shit figured out. I've been a fool. Maybe God didn't kill Doc, but he let it happen. Tell me, what kind of God is that?"

"Boy," Batty's voice was as firm as I had ever heard it. "You and I need to get some fresh air. Will you excuse us?" he asked Callie and Tom.

We slowly untangled ourselves from the little huddle that had formed around me on the floor of the hut. Batty and I made our way out the door.

"Callie and I will keep the fire going," Tom said, looking to Callie for agreement. She nodded consent.

Outside, Batty suggested that we walk down to the pond. He urged me to take a few deep breaths. The cold air burned my lungs, relieving the tightness in my chest, but not the lump in my throat.

"Chad, I've heard you say that Doc was the happiest person you had ever met. That true?" I managed to nod in agreement. He continued, "Haven't you wondered what he had that the rest of us are lacking?"

"It obviously had something to do with his faith," I answered.

"Son, it had everything to do with his faith. According to Doc, most folks suffer from limited horizons. That's your problem, Chad. Your horizon is limited."

Batty stopped in the middle of the path, which was not as worn as the one from the clearing to the hut, and motioned for me to look down. He kicked at a weed that had been withered by the same recent frost that had sapped the color from the trees. "See this weed? You've never seen a plant grow so fast as it does during summer. But its roots are very shallow. When the frost comes, its life is over." Batty's swift kick separated the dead plant from its loose mooring and sent it flying through the air. "You remember Doc's spiritual biology lesson, don't you? What did you learn?" Batty asked.

I fumbled for words, still looking at the spot where the weed had landed. "Yeah," I said, only half interested in pursuing the conversation. "See where that weed landed, Batty? It's lying on top of what looks like another dead weed, but that weed isn't dead."

"Well it looks like they're both dead to me," Batty observed.

I almost smiled when I realized that he was just playing along. "It's your limited horizon, Batty."

He feigned a look of surprise. We stopped where the two plants lay together. "What you don't see is that this second plant actually has a stem running underground," I continued, giving it the same kind of kick that Batty had administered to the first weed. The weed lost a few leaves, but otherwise held its ground. I kicked some earth away from the weed to reveal the root-like stem running underground. "This plant has a source of life which isn't visible. It is connected to this underground stem that gives it life even when its visible parts can no longer sustain it. This plant is still living."

Batty knew that my mind was faster than the words I was uttering. He knew that I had already made the connection between the plant and Doc's life and death. He felt no compulsion to pursue the spiritual biology lesson further.

By now the short path had brought us to the pond's edge. Half in and half out of the water lay the little row boat that Callie and I had used the morning after I had proposed to her.

Batty stood facing the boat. He reached in his coat pocket and pulled out a folded paper. He unfolded it, stared at it for a moment, looked out and surveyed the lake. I was about to ask him what he was doing when he turned back toward me and burst into tears. I grabbed him in a bear hug. My chest filled. My only release was to join his weeping.

What Batty and I both knew in our heads about life and death had not yet worked its way into the depths of our understanding and the journey there was painful, very painful.

The Ark

"This is Doc's boat," Batty said, breaking our embrace and turning toward the pond to wipe the remaining tears from his face. I wanted to ask about the now crumpled piece of paper which had opened the floodgate of tears we had shared. It must be a note from Doc, I thought. I resisted and Batty placed it back into his pocket. He climbed in the little boat and took a seat, facing me.

"This is a very unlikely ark," I commented, nodding toward the name painted on the little craft's stern.

"Yeah," Batty answered. "That's the name Doc gave it. Did you know I made this boat for him?"

"No," I said. "But I'm not surprised. You're quite a craftsman, Batty." I thought of telling him the story of how Callie and I had used the boat, but my heart wasn't in it. Anyway, I knew Batty would have a story about *The Ark*.

"Chad, if I told you I could take you on a voyage that would offer you total fulfillment and bring you to a destination filled with unimaginable reward, would you sign on board?"

"Well, I'd have to think about that. What would be the risks? What would be the consequences of staying on shore?"

"Oh, you don't have a choice of staying on shore, this is the sea of life," Batty explained, spreading his arms to draw my attention to the expanse of the mill pond. "Your only choice is how you'll make the trip to the other side."

"What other choices of transportation do I have?" I asked.

"Oh, other boats will come along to offer you passage. There are far more attractive and popular means of transportation," Batty answered. "But," he paused, "this is the only ark."

I turned up the collar on my jacket against the wind and climbed aboard. "On a hot summer's day, I might just wait for a better offer," I said. "but today this looks like my best choice."

Batty paused to allow me to settle in the other seat facing him. Then he spoke, "Yeah, it's conditions like these that coax most folks into *The Ark*." He fastened the oars in place and began to row.

"Doc and I have logged many a mile together in this little vessel," he said reflectively. "Doc told me just before he passed that he had plans to give you a ride in this *Ark*." He stopped rowing a moment and looked out over the water.

"Chad, do you know what an ark is?"

"Well, I know about Noah's Ark. He saved his family and all the animals from the flood in it."

Batty continued, "Do you remember that Moses' sister put him in an ark made of bulrushes to save him from Pharaoh's death squads?"

"I didn't know that was called an ark," I replied.

"Yeah, and there's at least one more ark mentioned in the Bible. But, it wasn't a boat at all. Do you know it?"

"I must have missed Sunday School that week, Batty. I don't know of another ark," I replied.

"Well, it's not really a kid's story like the other two," Batty continued. "But when Moses was leading the Jews toward the promised land, God had them build an ark. He instructed them to use the ark to carry the stone tablets on which Moses had recorded the Ten Commandments. The Jews eventually used it to carry the tablets and some other sacred items with them across the Jordan River into the promised land. Those three examples ought to give you some clue about what an ark is," Batty said and waited for me to answer.

"Well," I deduced, "they each carried a special cargo. And they each had to make it past some threat or obstacle. I would say an ark is a vessel used to transport precious cargo over or past some great obstacle."

"Exactly right, Chad. A vessel used to carry precious cargo over or past some great obstacle," Batty repeated, seeming to like my words better than those he would have chosen. "Hold that thought, Chad."

As we talked, Batty stroked the oars, to set the craft on one course, only to switch to another, and still another. After each change of course, he would lift his head and gaze at the tree line. The little craft cut cleanly through the choppy waters. The chilly air was sobering.

At every moment of silence, my mind flowed back to Doc's death like water seeking its lowest point. It was an effort to carry on conversation.

Near the middle of the pond, Batty withdrew the oars, laying them in their resting place inside *The Ark*. He blew warm breath on his freed hands and lifted the collar of his jacket against the stiff breeze that hit him in the face. The wake lapping against the little ark starkly contrasted this excursion with the glassy ride Callie and I had enjoyed. He removed the crumpled paper from his pocket and gave it a quick glance. He seemed satisfied and returned the paper to his pocket.

I couldn't resist. "Batty, what are you doing?"

"Navigating," was his one-word answer. "Chad, the past week or so has been an emotional roller coaster for you, hasn't it?

I mean, what with your marriage plans and now Doc's death." He paused, but did not wait for answer. "If you think about it, the happiest times and the saddest times we all experience in life involve relationships. Newly-formed relationships, deepening relationships, broken relationships, separations, homecomings, death. That's because relationship is the essence of life. Remember, it was Doc's definition for life.

"Tell me truthfully now, Chad. When did your relationship with Callie start to improve?" Batty asked, again knowing the answer before he spoke. This time, however, he waited for my answer.

"Well," I knew the answer too, but the cold air made the words hard to form. "The first thing that changed was my relationship with God. Really, that was when all my relationships changed. My relationship with Callie, of course. But, also my relationships with other people and even to the things around me. I just haven't seen things or people the same since Doc helped me find a real relationship with God. At least until now. I must admit, Doc's death has clouded a lot of things for me."

"And do you think all of those things or people suddenly changed?" Batty asked rhetorically. "Not really, Chad, it was your horizon that changed. You saw Callie differently because your vantage point had changed. The same thing happened to Jesus Christ. His unique relationship with his Father gave him the advantage of seeing this world, its things and its people, like no other human could see them."

"I couldn't agree more, Batty, but where are we going with this conversation?"

Batty responded, "Chad, until a short while ago, you were one of those folks looking for a means of transportation across this sea of life. Most times you probably felt like you were dead in the water. Perhaps being blown around with each change of wind. But, when you decided to establish a relationship with God, it was like God reached out His Spirit and helped you into His Ark. You and God's Spirit were in His Ark together. At first the waters seemed as smooth as glass. But now, for the first time since you climbed aboard, a storm has blown up and the sea of relationships is raging. Your relationship with the man who encouraged you to climb aboard has been severed and you are wondering if this vessel is seaworthy."

Just then, the wind began gusting so that the little craft rocked sideways. I grabbed both sides as if that would stop the swaying. Batty had to use the oars to bring *The Ark* back on course.

"Chad, in times like these, you need to remember that this is no ordinary boat, this is God's Ark. As long as you don't abandon ship, you'll have God's Spirit with you. And God is not about to lose his precious cargo, no matter how rough the sea becomes. That includes the fiercest of all storms…death.

"Son, I've been on the sea of life a lot longer than you have. I can tell you that the waters are going to get much rougher than they are today. The loss of Doc is very painful for all of us whose lives he touched. But there will be other days more personally trying than this one. Still, as long as you're in the *ark*, you are a part of God's precious cargo, which He will not abandon."

Batty took one of the oars from the metal sleeve again and gently stroked the water. *The Ark* accepted its new course. Then he continued, "Some people think that getting into the ark sentences them to a life of hard work at the oars. Not so. God supplies the power. But, we do have a job. He only asks us to stay seated in the boat and keep the ark on the course he has set. I mean by this that the most important work we do in life is to maintain our relationship with the ship's Captain.

"Sometimes, when our human relationships don't follow our personal expectations, we blame the other party, or God.

The real blame, however, needs to be laid at our own feet, with our own expectations. Wasn't this true with you and Callie?"

I nodded my agreement and Batty continued. "At times, it becomes necessary to verify our bearings, to realign the one basic relationship that changes all the others." Batty dipped the oar into the water and again the tiny craft responded by changing direction ever so slightly.

"That's really your problem with Doc's death, isn't it," Batty continued. "This is probably the first time that your expectations about a relationship with someone have been altered by death."

"Yeah," I agreed. "My grandparents died when I was very young. I never stood face-to-face with death. But Doc, he meant so much to me. He changed my life."

"No, Chad, God changed your life. Doc was a catalyst, like he was for me and for Tom and for many others, but the real change came when you began a new relationship with God. Son, what I'm trying to say is, whenever you allow other relationships to take your eyes off of the primary relationship of life, your horizon changes. Doc's death has temporarily knocked you off course. But, you mustn't let it change your destination."

Batty changed sides with the oar, stroking a couple of times rather vigorously. I hadn't noticed, but the course Batty had us on was leading directly toward a thicket along the shore line opposite the hut. Batty's back was to the thicket. I motioned for him to look, but he was now re-absorbed in the conversation.

"You see, Chad..."

"Batty, we're going to hit the shore!" I yelled. "Watch where you're going!" My alarm did not faze Batty. It was too late anyway. The little craft gave a heave upward, the stern spun and *The Ark* dipped downward. I grabbed both sides of the boat and ducked to avoid being decapitated in the thicket. Without raising my head, I looked for Batty. He had not seen the approaching danger.

The Ark made a complete 360-degree turn, but we were still afloat. My eyes caught sight of Batty. He was sitting upright in the middle of the boat with his arms wrapped around his middle to help contain his laughter. I slowly lifted my head and looked Batty straight in the eye. "You old codger, what do you mean scaring me to death? What did you do? Where are we?"

Batty just kept on chuckling as his arms went spread-eagle and his body twisted from side to side. "Where do you think we are?" he yelled. "We're in Heaven!"

The Ark continued its slow spin, giving us a panorama of a secluded lagoon. It was obviously connected to the pond. But beyond that, there were few similarities, at least on this day. The killing frost had not found the trees that surrounded the still waters. Their leaves were brilliant with color, intensified by the rays of the late evening sun that until now had not shown its face this whole day. The wind did not penetrate the thicket. I supposed it was the contrast that made this place feel warm.

"Wow!" I exclaimed. "How did this happen?"

Batty had now contained his laughter. He scratched his head in feigned puzzlement. "Beats me. I just followed the charted course and we ended up here."

"What course? Have you been here before?"

The old black man's voice softened. "Nope, can't say as I have. I've been told about it. My grandpappy first told me such a place existed long ago, but I never had the guts to put his instructions to the test. Then a few weeks ago, something Doc Masters said reminded me of the old story. Doc and I had planned to take this trip together soon. Now, with things changed and all...I just figured it was time we both learned this lesson."

I spoke, "Well, now that we've had the experience, will you please explain the lesson?"

"Not now, son. I'm not through appreciating the experience."

From that point, the only sound was the musical accompaniment of birds who were resting in this safe haven. Batty moved his head slowly from side to side. Occasionally, he would lift his face to the sky and his eyes would close, forcing tears to traverse his wrinkled face and neck until they disappeared beneath his collar.

I inhaled deeply, trying, I suppose, to crowd every corpuscle of my being with the delight of these moments. The peace I felt settled gently into the emptiness created by Doc's death.

Time did not enter our consciousness until the reddened evening sky began to give way to darkness. "Batty," I asked, "what is Heaven really like?"

Before answering, he took a long look around the earthly heaven that surrounded us. "Well, son, that's the sixty-four dollar question, ain't it? To me, it's kind of like comparing the pond out there with this small piece of paradise. Heaven is what we wish earth could be."

"And what would that be for you, Batty?" I asked.

His response was immediate. "For me it would be a perfect relationship with everybody and everything around me. After all, if relationships define life, then perfect relationships must define eternal life.

"Chad, do you remember how you felt when you first knew that you and Callie were going to spend your lives together? I'll bet everything around you seemed, well, perfect." I smiled in confirmation. "That experience probably comes as close as any to being what Doc is experiencing now that he realizes that he is going to spend eternity with God. It's the glow of that relationship which will create the perfection in all that will be around us in heaven.

"Son, there's a lot more I could tell you about my concept of heaven, but it's going to be dark in just a little while. We had better find our way back to the pond while there is still some light."

Batty used the oar to move *The Ark* to a small clearing on shore, explaining that we could not return the way we came. We disembarked and pulled *The Ark* over and through some brush. It only took a short while to reach the pond again. Batty took his seat at the oars despite my offer to row back to the hut.

"No," Batty insisted, "you need to have the view I had on the trip over here. You won't have any view for long, so let me point something out to you. Here, take this piece of paper."

Batty handed me the crumpled paper from his pocket. I hastily stuffed it into my jacket while I launched the tiny craft with a running push, and then hopped aboard.

Batty was right, the only light remaining was in the western sky beyond the hut. The darkness had replaced the winds with a blanket of dampness that intensified the cold. I retrieved the paper, zipped my jacket to the top and warmed my hands between my legs, holding the paper for further instructions.

"Look over my right shoulder at about tree level," Batty instructed. "What do you see?"

"Well," I thought out loud, "there's a distinct contrast between the tree line and the red sky beyond. It creates a kind of silhouette. And, there are a couple of trees towering over the others. That's all I see, Batty."

"Yes," he confirmed. "that's all there is to see. Describe the two tall trees to me."

"Okay, the one nearest the pond looks like a cypress. It has a funny top. It actually forms a 'Y'," I said, using my hands and arms to illustrate. "It looks like a sling shot. And the other tree seems to be behind the cypress. I would say it's a pine. Its straight trunk extends almost directly through the center of the sling shot."

Batty assessed my description without turning to face the scene. I see you even learned a little botany from Doc Masters. You're right about the kind of trees. Tell me what you see on the paper I gave you."

I glanced at a crude drawing on the paper. As crude as it first appeared, the drawing was almost an exact copy of what my eyes had beheld on the horizon. My face must have shown my surprise.

Batty gave me a big knowing smile and said, "Tell me what it would take to line up the pine tree directly inside the sling shot angle as it appears on the drawing."

I leaned my body to the left, which caused the pine to appear to center itself like a builder's level. "There, move *The Ark* a little to your right," I said.

Batty stopped rowing. He used one oar as a rudder to move *The Ark* as I had directed. I straightened back up to confirm the centering. "Steady as she goes, matey. Keep her dead on that course," I said in a nautical voice.

That got a chuckle from Batty. "You're probably way ahead of me, Chad. If so, you know now how I guided us to the secret lagoon. Grandpappy told me that the old folks at Piney Grove Church knew our little secret. The preacher and some deacons laid out the church house over in the clearing so that the steeple would line up in the angle of that old cypress. The old timers said that's what they used to guide on. I guess I'm one of the few folks that even remembered the old stories about the place they called heaven. 'Course, since the church house burned down, nobody really knew the way, including me. But Doc and I figured that the old timers must have had some reference point before the steeple stood there. For the life of us, we could not discover what it was. Chad, look at that piece of paper again. Look real close."

"It's uncanny how closely the drawing resembles reality," I remarked as I studied the crumpled drawing. Where did you get this map?"

"I'll say it's uncanny," Batty responded. "What else do you see on that sheet?"

"There's a logo on the top. It says University Hospital."

"Chad, Doc drew that on his deathbed. His vocal cords were damaged by one of those bullets and his energy was almost completely drained. But he had the biggest smile on his face when he sketched that map. When he finished, Doc just nodded to me and closed his piercing, blind eyes."

Batty swallowed hard and then continued, "I never had to find the hidden opening with my own eyes. I only needed to know the guidance system and exercise a little faith. Frankly, I was as surprised as you were when we went down and around like we did. But the difference was that my surprise was accompanied by delight because I knew where we were headed. You were afraid because you had no prior knowledge of anything beyond the shoreline. We had different horizons and that made all the difference."

"That's true, Batty. You did scare the wits out of me. But I did reach the same destination, didn't I?"

"Sure, boy," Batty barked. "But you were with me. In life, every person must pilot his own vessel. There is no room for another crew member. Unless of course, you can find a first mate that doesn't occupy any space. You know what I mean?

"That's the problem in the world today, Chad. There are all kinds of new boats on the sea of life nowadays. All of 'em promising smooth sailing. But they all lack the same thing. They don't really have a destination beyond the horizon. It's precisely beyond the horizon that this world's hope lies. Somebody has got to keep passing on the map."

The last light of day allowed me to see Batty's white teeth shining through his mile-wide grin. He picked up the pace of his rowing. "You got any idea how we can find the hut, Chad?" he asked.

I looked toward where I thought it might be. Tom and Callie had hung out a lantern. It provided all the navigational aid we needed. We pulled *The Ark* up on shore, tied her to a small tree and made our way up the path to the hut.

The warmth of the fire inside the hut and Callie's open arms welcomed me home. Tom gave Batty the same treatment, well, almost the same treatment. We removed our jackets and spread our hands in front of the wood stove. Callie offered us each a can of Cheerwine left over from an S.O.B.'s meeting. Batty waved it away. I popped the top on one for old times' sake. It fizzed over the side and made my hand sticky, but the warm wetness felt good to my dry throat.

Callie spoke, "We thought we were going to have to get the dragnet out to find you two. Where have you been?

Batty's eyes met mine as if to say you might want to save this story until another time. I simply smiled and answered Callie. "I'll show you someday after we're married." It was probably the thought of our being married, but my answer seemed to suffice. Callie just shrugged and gave me another hug.

Tom changed the subject. "Folks, it's late and Batty and I have an errand to run. Doc asked us to pay that young man at the city jail a visit. But first, I have a little business to attend to right here. You two come over here where there's more light." He meant Callie and me. Batty stayed over by the door.

Tom explained, "Last week, Doc Masters asked me to handle a little real estate transaction for him. Chad, he knew that this place was where you found your faith and where the two of you really found each other. So, he thought it would make an appropriate wedding gift." He handed us a document with a legal cover which had Callie's name and mine on it. It read, 'Deed and Release.'

I held up the papers between my face and Tom's. "What is this, Tom?" I asked in disbelief.

"Just what it says," he replied. "It's a deed to this hut...and, of course the land and pond that goes with it. You need to know that this property was the last worldly possession Doc had. He told me to tell you two that he figured your life together might take you to many other places. You are welcome to do with the property what you wish. But he hoped you would always remember the love you first found here."

"But what about you, Tom, or Batty? You deserve this property," Callie protested.

"Doc knew I have no need for another piece of property and Batty would just waste away his life fishing," Tom said, winking in Batty's direction.

"We'll be glad to look after the place if you two wind up moving out of town," Batty added. Tom and I would like to keep the Society meetings going if you don't mind."

We nodded in agreement. Callie and I hugged the two old men. Tom pushed Batty out the door and bent low to avoid the door casing on his way through.

Outside, he turned back to face Callie and me, and swung the lantern from side to side. "You had better come ahead, this is the only light we have."

I quickly shut the damper on the old stove and assisted Callie through the door. We followed a few feet behind Tom and

Batty until we all made the clearing. They left the lantern at our feet and moved ahead toward the Buick, aided now only by the moonlight.

Tom and Batty talked quietly. Still, we could easily hear them in the quiet night. The damp air gave off the smell of burned umbers from the ruins of the old church. Batty stumbled slightly on what appeared to be the old front steps, but Tom caught his fall. Batty righted himself and gave a little chuckle.

Batty spoke to Tom as they walked toward the Buick. "It's a funny thing, those steps just reminded me of the dog that got religion. Did I ever tell you about the time, years ago, that these folks came to Piney Grove one Sunday morning? Their little dog jumped out of their car, ran up those same steps and straight down the aisle. I'll never forget that sight! The Spirit must have got ahold of him."

I stopped in my tracks as the two S.O.B.'s pulled off in the Buick. I was stunned. I simply couldn't believe my ears. Callie looked questioningly into my tear-blinded eyes. She must have felt my shivering through our clenched hands.

We stood in that place for a very long time, staring at the charred remains of the old church, saying nothing, holding hands. All three of us.